# RESCUED BY THE SINGLE DAD DOC

## MARION LENNOX

MILLS & BOON

First published in Great Britain 2019
by Mills & Boon, an imprint of HarperCollins*Publishers*
1 London Bridge Street, London, SE1 9GF

Large Print edition 2020

© 2019 Marion Lennox

ISBN: 978-0-263-08568-6

MIX
Paper from
responsible sources
FSC
www.fsc.org    FSC® C007454

This book is produced from independently certified FSC™ paper to ensure responsible forest management. For more information visit www.harpercollins.co.uk/green.

Printed and bound in Great Britain
by CPI Group (UK) Ltd, Croydon, CR0 4YY

**Marion Lennox** has written over one hundred romance novels, and is published in over one hundred countries and thirty languages. Her international awards include the prestigious RITA® Award (twice!) and the *RT Book Reviews* Career Achievement Award for 'a body of work which makes us laugh and teaches us about love'. Marion adores her family, her kayak, her dog, and lying on the beach with a book someone else has written. Heaven!

With thanks to Mary Michele,
whose kindness made this book
so much easier.

This book is for Denise,
who, with her wobbly mate Molly,
helps make this place home.

# CHAPTER ONE

DR RACHEL TILDING enjoyed treating kids. If they couldn't speak it was often up to Rachel to figure out what was wrong, but in general kids' needs were uncomplicated. They didn't intrude on her personal space. If all Rachel's patients were kids—without parents—she might well be looking at a different career path.

As it was, her aim was to be a radiologist, interpreting results from state-of-the-art equipment and having little to do with patients at all. But the terms of her scholarship specified she had to spend her first two years after internship as a family doctor in Shallow Bay. She'd geared herself to face it.

What she hadn't prepared herself for was living next to a house full of kids. Their noise was bad enough, plus the yips of excitement from their dog. Then, a mere two hours after she'd moved in, a ball smashed through her window, almost making her drop the carton of glassware she'd been unpacking. The ball landed in a spray of shattered glass in the kitchen sink.

Count to ten, she told herself. These are kids. Don't yell.

She'd been telling herself that since she'd arrived. These were her new neighbours. It wasn't their fault that she valued privacy above all else. Someone would call them in for dinner soon. They'd go to bed and she'd have the silence she craved.

But kids as such close neighbours…

Shallow Bay's nurse-manager had sent her pictures of this little house, a pretty-as-a-picture cottage surrounded by bushland. A five-minute walk took her up to the Shallow Bay Hospital, and five minutes in the other direction took her down to the beach.

What the pictures hadn't shown, however, was that it was one of three cottages, huddled together in the dip before the bay. Hers was the smallest. The largest was the middle one and that seemed to be filled with boys.

She wasn't sure how many yet. The noise they were making could have denoted a small army. She'd been trying to figure how she could intervene without turning Shallow Bay's new doctor into Dragon Lady.

Now she had no choice. A cricket ball was sitting in her kitchen sink, surrounded by a spray of glass.

But before she could react, a shock of curly red hair appeared at the shattered window. Underneath the hair were two huge green eyes, fear-filled. The window was high for a child, so he'd obviously hoisted himself up to see where his ball had landed.

The head disappeared and a hand appeared in its place. And groped into the sink. Through shattered glass.

'No!' She'd been standing behind packing boxes on the far side of the table. She launched herself across the kitchen, but the groping hand reached the ball before she did.

There was a yelp of pain and then hand and ball disappeared.

She hauled the back door open, raced down the steps and cut the child off before he could back away. He'd lurched back from the window and was staggering.

'Don't move!' Her order contained all the authority of a doctor who'd spent her two years of internship working in emergency medicine. The child froze, staring down at his hand in horror.

Their little dog, a black and white terrier—a ball of pseudo-aggression—came tearing across the lawn and barked hysterically, as if it was Rachel who was the intruder on her own lawn.

It had…three legs?

'Tuffy! Tuffy, back. He won't bite. Please… Kit's just getting our ball.' The voice from the far side of the hedge sounded terrified. The oldest child?

They were all redheads. The two on the far side of the hedge looked about ten and six. The child under her window was maybe eight.

They all had huge green eyes. Pale skin with freckles. They all looked rigid with fear.

Maybe her voice had done that to them. Even the little dog was backing away.

Was she so scary?

Rachel had little to do with kids except as patients, but the middle child was now definitely a patient. He was still clutching the ball, but he was holding it out in front of him. A line of crimson was dripping onto the garden bed.

'Don't move,' she said again, because the child was looking in panic across to his brothers—

they had to be brothers—and she knew his instinct was to run. 'I'm not angry.' Okay, maybe she was, but this wasn't the time to admit it. There'd be an adult somewhere, responsible for leaving this group unsupervised. They deserved a piece of her mind, not this child. One thing Rachel was very careful about—a lesson learned from the long years of an unjust childhood—was that fairness was everything.

'You've cut your hand on the glass,' she told the little boy as she reached him. She took his arm and raised it, applying pressure around the wrist. 'You need to stay still.'

The eyes that looked up at her were huge. He looked terrified. There'd be pain. With this much blood, it had to be deep. The blood wasn't pumping—the radial artery must surely be intact—but the gash from multiple glass shards tentacled out from wrist to palm. In a child, this amount of bleeding could well lead to collapse.

'I'm a doctor,' she told him, gentling her voice. 'The glass has cut your hand, but we can fix it. Right now, though, it's looking messy, so we need to stop it bleeding. You'll feel better if you don't look at it until we've cleaned it up. Look at your brothers, or look at the hole in my window. That's quite a hole.'

She was manoeuvring his hand upward, edging her body to block his gaze. The ball fell to the ground as she lifted his hand high, curling his palm in slightly so the hand created its own pressure on the pierced palm. There could well be shards of glass in there but now wasn't the time to remove them. She needed a surgery, equipment, help.

'Can you run inside and get your mum or dad?' she called to the two boys on the far side of the hedge. 'Ask them to bring out a towel. Run!

'Tell me your name,' she asked the little boy.

She got a blank look in response. Fear.

'He's Christopher,' the elder of the pair behind the hedge called. 'But we call him Kit. Are you really a doctor?'

'I am. Could you fetch your parents please? Now! Kit needs your help.'

'We don't have parents. Just a stepfather.'

*Just a stepfather.*

Why did that make her freeze?

The wave of nausea that swept through her was as vicious as it was dumb. Her past was just that—past—and it had no place here, now.

Somehow, she managed to fight back the bile rising in her throat, to haul herself together, to become the responsible person these boys needed.

She needed a plan.

She needed a responsible adult to help her.

Her phone was inside. Where had she put it? Somewhere in the muddle of unpacked goods?

She daren't let Kit's arm go to find it herself. He was too big for her to pick up and carry. He was also looking increasingly pale. Had these kids been left on their own?

'Where's your stepfather now?' she asked, and stupidly she heard the echoes of her dumb, visceral response to the word in her voice.

'At work,' the eldest boy told her.

'Is there anyone else here?'

'Christine's inside, watching telly.'

'Then fetch her,' she ordered. 'Fast. Tell her Kit's hurt his hand and he's bleeding. Tell her I need a towel and a phone. Run.'

'Can you just put a plaster on it?' the older boy asked. 'We don't want to tell Christine. She'll tell Tom.'

'What's your name?'

'Marcus. And this is Henry. Please don't tell.

If we misbehave, Tom'll make us go back to our grandparents.'

'You haven't misbehaved. The ball broke my window, not you,' she told him. She'd tell him anything he liked to get help right now. 'Marcus, this cut is too big for a plaster. Kit needs Christine. I need Christine. Run.'

He shouldn't have left the boys with Christine. Normally Tom Lavery used his next-door neighbour, Rose, as childminder. Rose was in her seventies, huge-hearted, reliable. The boys loved her, but this morning she'd fallen and hurt her hip. It was only bruised, thank heaven, but she needed rest.

This weekend was also the annual field-day-cum-funfair at Ferndale, two hours' drive across the mountains. For the isolated town of Shallow Bay, the Ferndale Show was huge. Practically the entire population took part, with cattle parades and judging, baking competitions, kids' activities. As Shallow Bay emptied, Christine, Rose's niece, had become his childminder of last resort.

'Worrying?' Roscoe, Shallow Bay's hospital nurse administrator, was watching Tom from the far side of the nurses' station. Tom was supposed to be filling in patient histories. Instead he'd turned to the window, looking down towards the cottage.

'Go home and check,' Roscoe said. For a big man—make that huge—Roscoe was remarkably perceptive. 'You'll be writing Bob up for antacids instead of antibiotics if you're not careful.'

'I'm careful.' He hauled his attention back to his job. 'Christine can cope.'

'As long as there's no ad for hair curlers on telly. You know she's a dipstick,' Roscoe said bluntly.

Roscoe's smile was half hidden by his beard, but it didn't hide the sympathy. 'Go home, doc,' he told him again. 'I'll ring you if I need you, and I'll drop these charts off for you to fill in after the boys go to sleep tonight. I wish you could be taking the boys across to Ferndale, but hey, you have another doctor here on Monday. All problems solved, no?'

No, Tom thought as he snagged the next chart and started writing. It was all very well for Roscoe to say he could do these tonight, but if he fell behind in his paperwork he'd never catch up.

Another hour...

But he glanced at the window one last time. The boys were capable of anything.

For what was maybe the four thousandth time over the last two years he thought, What have I let myself in for?

How long's for ever?

And then his attention was diverted. There was a car speeding up the track from the bay. A scarlet roadster. A two-seater.

Tom's cottage was one of only three down that road. Few people used it except for Tom, Rose and Rose's occasional visitors.

And the new doctor? He'd been told she'd collected the key from Reception a couple of hours back. Poppy, the junior nurse who'd given her the key, had been frustratingly vague when asked for a description. 'Quite old, really,' she'd said, which in Poppy's twenty-two-year-old eyes meant anything over twenty-three. 'And ordinary. Just, you know, dullsville when it comes to clothes. Didn't say much, just took the key and said she'd be at work at nine on Monday. She drives a cool car, though.'

If this was it, it certainly was cool, a streamlined beauty, the kind of car Tom used to love to drive—in another life.

So this would be Rachel Tilding, the new doctor, the latest of the Lavery Scholarship recipients, here to pay her dues with two years' service. He imagined she'd be heading to the shops to buy supplies or a takeaway meal for dinner. He should drop over tonight to say hi.

But tonight he didn't have his normal backup of Rose, who was always ready to slip over and mind the kids whenever he needed to go out. He could scarcely go over bearing wine and casserole and say, Welcome to Shallow Bay. Plus, he was dead tired. If he had the energy to make a casserole there'd be no way it'd leave his house.

He sighed and started to turn back to the desk—but then he paused. The car had turned off the road and was heading down the hospital driveway.

He could make the driver out now. The woman seemed slight, fair-skinned, with brown curly hair tumbling to her shoulders. Leaning against her was a child.

A child with his arm raised, caught in some sort of sling. An arm which was bright crimson.

*Kit!*

Running in hospitals was forbidden. From training it was instilled into you. No matter the

emergency, walking swiftly gets you there almost as fast, with far less likelihood of causing
another emergency.

Stuff training. Dr Tom Lavery ran.

She'd collected this gorgeous little car three
weeks ago and she still practically purred every
time she looked at it. Two years of internship,
living in hospital accommodation and being constantly tired, meant that she'd spent practically
nothing of her two years' wages. The condition
of the scholarship which had funded her training
meant she was now facing two years of 'exile' in
the country. This car would be a gift to herself,
she'd decided, to celebrate being a fully quali-
fied doctor with her internship behind her. It'd
also be something to remind her of the life she'd
have when she could finally return to the city.

She'd driven it to Shallow Bay with a beam on
her face a mile wide, blocking out the thought
that she'd had to hire a man with a van to bring
her possessions, as nothing bigger than a de-
signer suitcase would fit in with her.

But now she wasn't thinking of her car. She
had a child in her passenger seat, a little boy so
white she thought he was about to pass out. She'd

put as much pressure as she dared on his arm, slinging it roughly upward before somehow managing to carry him to her car. Her cream leather was turning scarlet to match the paintwork. Any minute now Kit could throw up. Or, worse, lose consciousness.

Please, no. She loved this car but if she had the choice between vomit or coma...

'Hold on, Kit,' she muttered. The decision to get him to the hospital rather than calling for an ambulancc had been instantaneous. He still had glass in his hand. The blood he'd lost was frightening and the hospital was so close...

'I want Tom,' he quavered.

Tom? His stepfather? That was the name the kids had used. And Christine? The overblown, overpainted woman had emerged from the house, taken one look and fled back inside, saying, 'I'll ring Tom.' So much for practical help. Rachel had hauled off her own windcheater and used that as a pressure bandage and sling.

'Tell Christine—and Tom—I've taken him to the hospital,' she'd told his terrified brothers, and then she'd left. There was time for nothing else.

'We'll find Tom,' she told Kit now, as he slumped against her. 'But first we need to stop your hand bleeding. We can do this, Kit. Be brave. Isn't it lucky I'm a doctor?'

The sight that met him as he emerged from the Emergency entrance was horrific. All he could see was blood. And one small boy.

For a moment he felt as if his legs might give way. Kit's face, his hair, his T-shirt, were soaked with blood. The T-shirt was a treasured one, covered with meerkat cartoons. Tom couldn't see a single meerkat now, though. All he could see was blood.

*Kit.*

'Mate, you're doctor first, stepdad second.' It was Roscoe, placing a huge palm on his shoulder as they both headed for the car. 'Right now, Kit needs a doctor.'

The words steadied him but only a little. He reached the car and hauled the door open.

Kit was leaning heavily against the driver. Had she hit him? A car accident? What…?

'Lacerated hand.' The woman's voice cut across his nightmare, her voice as incisive, as firm as Roscoe's. 'From a broken window. No other injury, but severe blood loss. I suspect there'll still be glass in there. His name's Kit and he's asking for Tom.'

'Kit.' His voice sounded as if it came from a long way away. Kit was struggling to look at him, struggling to focus. 'T-Tom...' he managed—and then his eyes rolled back and he lost consciousness.

*Kit!*

It was Roscoe who took over. For those first appalling seconds—and it must only have been seconds—Tom froze, but Roscoe's voice boomed across the entrance, calling back into the Emergency ward behind. 'Trolley,' he boomed. 'IV. Blood loss, people. Move.'

And then as Barry, their elderly hospital orderly, came scuttling out with the trolley, and Jenny, their second most senior nurse, appeared with the crash cart, Tom recovered enough to scoop Kit out of the car.

Somehow Tom's years of training kicked in. Triage. Look past the obvious. Get the facts and get them fast.

The woman had been wedged between Kit and the driver's door. She looked almost as gory as the child. Thirtyish. Jeans. Long shirt, bloodstained. A smear of blood on her face.

'Are you hurt yourself?' he managed.

'No,' she snapped, hauling herself out of the car. 'Just the child.'

Jenny had the crash cart beside him. With this amount of blood loss, cardiac arrest was a terrifying possibility.

'I'm a doctor,' the woman said. 'Rachel Tilding. Who's senior here?'

She was asking because he wasn't acting like a doctor. Roscoe, Barry, Jenny all looked in control. Not him.

He made a huge effort and hauled himself back into his professional self. Terror was still there but it was on the backburner, waiting to surface when there was time.

'IV,' he managed, laying Kit on the trolley. The little boy's hand had been roughly put in a sling to hold it high.

A doctor…

*What had she done to Kit?*

'It's only his hand.' She was out of the car now, moving swiftly around to the trolley. 'He smashed my window with a cricket ball, then reached in to try and get it.'

Only his hand…but this amount of blood?

'Straight to Theatre?' Roscoe demanded.

'Yes,' she snapped back at Roscoe. 'I'll help if there's no one else. I don't know about parents. I didn't have time to find out. Just this Tom…'

'I'm Tom,' he said heavily. 'I'm his stepfather. He's my responsibility.'

'Stepfather…' She glanced at him in stupefaction. 'What sort of a…?' And then she collected herself. 'No matter. Kit needs a doctor, now.'

'I'm a doctor. Tom Lavery.'

'What the…you're working as a doctor and employing that…that…'

She obviously couldn't find a word to describe Christine. Neither could he. Maybe there wasn't one, but he and Christine were obviously grouped together. Dr Tilding's look said Tom's position in the hierarchy of life on earth was somewhere below pond scum.

'Never mind,' she snapped. 'You can give me all the excuses in the world after we've seen to Kit's hand. Let's get him to Theatre. Now.'

# CHAPTER TWO

AND THEN THINGS reassembled themselves. Sort of. This was a small country hospital but it was geared for emergencies, and many emergencies involved rapid blood loss.

Kit had lost so much that cardiac arrest was still a real possibility. Treatment of his hand—apart from stemming the bleeding—had to wait until that threat was past.

And in Rachel he had a godsend. She was an angry godsend, judgemental and furious, but she was a doctor.

Maybe he could have coped alone—maybe—but he was acting on autopilot. A part of his brain seemed to have frozen. The sight of one little boy, unconscious, a child he'd learned to love, had knocked him sideways.

It was an insidious thing, this love. It had crept up and caught him unawares, and loving came with strings. He couldn't care for these kids—and love them—without his heart being wrenched, over and over again.

It was lurching now, sickeningly, and after that one incredulous look, that one outburst of anger, Rachel had subtly taken control.

As he went to put in the IV line his hand shook, and she took the equipment from him. 'Get the monitors working,' she told him. 'I'll take over here.'

The cardiac monitors... He needed to set them up. He did, with speed. A shaking hand could manage pads and monitors.

'Pain relief and anaesthetic,' she said. 'Do you have an anaesthetist?'

'There's only me,' he told her.

'Two of us, then,' she said curtly. 'Or one and a half if you're emotionally involved. But I'm trusting you have a good nursing staff.'

'The best,' Roscoe growled, and she nodded acknowledgement. This was no time for false modesty and she obviously accepted it.

And then Kit's eyes flickered open again, fighting to focus. Falling on Rachel first. Terror came flooding back, and Rachel saw.

'Hey, we found your Tom,' she told him. 'And here he is.' Her anger and her judgement had obviously been set aside with the need for reassurance. She edged aside so the little boy could see him. 'Kit, we're going to fix your hand. The bleeding's made you feel funny, and I know it hurts, but we're giving you something that'll make you feel better really fast. Tom's just going to test your fingers. Will you do what he tells you?'

And she stepped back, turning to the instrument tray, setting the scene so Kit could only see Tom.

She was impelling him to steady. She was pushing him to do what he had to do.

He had to focus and somehow he did.

Appallingly, he was still seeing terror as well as pain in the little boy's eyes. Legacy of his ghastly grandparents?

'Hey, Kit, you're here now, with me,' he said as they rolled the trolley into Theatre. He touched the little boy's face, willing the fear to disappear. 'You've cut your hand but we'll fix it. I know it hurts, but we'll stop it hurting really soon.'

'I broke… You're not mad…?'

'Dr Rachel tells me you broke her window,' he managed. 'I broke four windows when I was your age. I used to tell my mum and dad the cat did it. They didn't believe me but they weren't mad and neither am I. Accidents happen. Kit, can you tell me what you feel when I touch your fingers? Can you press back when I press? Here? Here?'

He was now in professional mode—sort of—but the lurch in his stomach wasn't going away.

And the information he gained from Kit as they settled him into Theatre wasn't helping.

He was checking for damage to the tendons that ran through the palm and attached to the finger bones. Secondly, for nerve damage, which could result in permanent loss of function or sensation. Tom was applying gentle pressure to the tips of Kit's fingers, asking him to push back.

The responses weren't good.

And Rachel got it. She was focusing on the IV, on getting pain relief on board, but she was listening to Kit's quavering answers. Knowing what they meant.

'Okay, Dr Lavery, tell me the set-up,' she said as Tom's testing finished. 'Do you have anyone here who can cope with paediatric plastics? Or someone who can get here fast?'

'No,' he said shortly. Stemming the bleeding seemed straightforward. It looked as if the radial artery had been nicked—it must have been to cause this amount of bleeding. They could fix that. But what his examination had told them was that Kit needed a plastic surgeon or a vascular surgeon or both if he wasn't to lose part or all of the use of that hand.

That meant evacuation. It was eight hours by road to Melbourne, ten to Sydney or Canberra. Shallow Bay wasn't the most remote place in Australia but its position, nestled on the far south-east coast, surrounded by hundreds of miles of mountainous forests, meant that reaching skilled help could be a logistical nightmare.

'Where?' Rachel said, and he had to give her credit for incisiveness.

'Sydney.'

'You have air transfer?'

'It'll take medevac an hour to reach us in the chopper, but yes.'

'Can someone organise that?' she said to Roscoe. 'Now?' And then she turned back to the child she was treating and her voice gentled. 'Kit, we're going to get your hand bandaged now, and stop things hurting, but there's a bit of damage deep inside that might make your fingers not as strong as they should be. We need to take you to a big hospital to get your hand mended.'

'Tom can fix it.' Kit's voice quavered.

'He can,' she said, injecting her voice with confidence. 'I know that. And so can I, because Tom and I are both doctors. If Tom agrees, I'll do the first part now. But have you ever seen Tom sew something that's ripped? Like a pair of jeans?'

'He did once,' Kit managed, trying gamely to sound normal. 'Big stitches. It came apart again.'

'Hey, how did I guess?' she said, smiling down at him. 'So Tom's not very good at sewing and neither am I. Kit, there are things in your hand called tendons which make your fingers work. You've hurt them, so what you need is a doctor who's really good at tiny stitches. Don't worry, we'll give you something that stops you feeling what we need to do. We'll make sure nothing hurts, I promise. You'll end up with a neat scar you'll be able to show your friends, but a good needleworking doctor will make sure your fingers end up stronger than ever. So what that means is that we need to take you to Sydney.'

'I don't want to go.'

'I understand that,' Rachel said. 'I've just arrived at Shallow Bay and it looks a great place. But have you ever been in a helicopter?'

'I… No.'

'Then what an adventure. Your friends will be so jealous. Tom, will you be going with Kit, or is there someone he needs more?'

And she looked straight at him.

So did Kit.

*Is there someone he needs more?*

Her eyes were challenging. Angry? He didn't get the anger, but he couldn't afford to focus on it now.

Kit needs his mother, he thought, and it was the belief he'd had reinforced about a thousand times in the last two years. But Claire was dead.

Kit's father was who knew where? Steve had been Claire's folly. The responsibility was never going to be Steve's.

Kit's grandparents? Claire's parents? They'd glory in this drama. They'd use it against him and his fight for custody would start all over again.

So he had to go with Kit, but to leave Shallow Bay… To leave two more needy children…

'There's no one but me,' he said, and it nearly killed him to say it.

'We'll manage.' It was Roscoe, gruff, stern, decisive. 'You need to go, Doc. And hey, we have another doc here now.'

'But Marcus. Henry. I can't.'

'They can stay at home,' Roscoe told him. 'We'll find someone to stay with them.'

'Not that childminder.' When Rachel spoke to Kit she was gentleness itself but when she faced Tom he saw judgement that he'd left the kids with such a woman. 'She's unfit.'

'She's awful,' Kit quavered. 'I don't like her.'

'It's okay,' Tom said, feeling helpless. He took Kit's good hand and squeezed. 'I'll fix this.' But how?

'Their normal minder is Rose,' Roscoe told Rachel. 'She hurt her hip yesterday but she's great. The kids love her. She'll stay with them.'

'She can't,' Tom said, option after option being discarded with increasing desperation. 'Not by herself. Not with her hip, and I can't trust Christine to help her. And with the field day at Ferndale—how many people are free this weekend?' He sounded desperate—he knew he did—but he was torn in so many directions. Kit needed him, but so did Marcus and Henry. As a parent, he was failing on all counts.

'We'll find someone,' Roscoe said, but he was starting to sound unsure. He turned to Rachel, explaining Tom's dilemma for him. 'The annual show at Ferndale is a huge deal and almost all the locals go. There's an added problem, too. These kids have had a bit of a tough time in the past and they need to stay in their own beds. Farming them out's not an option. I'd offer but my wife's almost nine months pregnant. What if she goes into labour?'

'You can't do it,' she said bluntly. She was still looking at Tom as if he was something she'd found at the back of the fridge, something that had been mouldering for months. 'So who can these boys depend on?'

'Me,' Tom said bleakly.

'Which is why we have one child with a sliced hand and two children with no carer.'

'We'll find someone,' Roscoe said again, but Tom felt ill. Rachel's disdain was obvious and he deserved it. Who could he ask, given this amount of notice?

But the expression on Rachel's face had changed. She looked…as if she was about to step into a chasm? It was a momentary look and then her expression became one of resolution. As if a decision had been made, but the decision was scary.

'Okay, then,' she said briskly, as if what was about to be said needed to be said before she changed her mind. 'Decision. If there's no other option, I'll accept responsibility. The boys don't know me, but I'm dependable. I can't imagine you'll need to stay in Sydney for more than a couple of days.'

'I can't... They won't...'

'I'm not offering to do this on my own,' she said, still brisk. 'Nor should you agree if I did. There's no way you should trust me. But if Rose of the hurt hip is otherwise okay... Would she agree to stay with the boys to give them the security they need? If she's willing, then I'll stay too. I can do housework, anything physical, and I can care for Rose as well as the boys. I don't mind sleeping on the floor if I need to. I've had experience of living with kids. I can cope with anything they throw at me.'

'I can't ask that of you,' Tom said, but she skewered him with a look that said he needed to get his act together.

'So what are your options?'

There weren't any.

'Rachel, with Tom away, we'll be needing you as a doctor,' Roscoe said, sounding stunned. 'I know you're not supposed to start until Monday but there's no one else. You know our last doc left us in the lurch. She had one of those scholarships you're on, but bang, she got herself pregnant and her fiancée paid her way out. So there's only Tom. And now there's only you.'

Then his face cleared. 'But maybe it would work. Rose isn't disabled, just sore. She lives in the third cottage down on your bay and she's slept at Tom's before. There's a spare bedroom, and I imagine you could use Tom's bed. There's an intercom from Tom's living room to the nurses' station here, so someone can always listen in if you need to be at the hospital. That works if Tom has to fix a drip or something at three in the morning. Tom works around his family. I guess you can, too.'

'I guess I can,' Rachel said.

'I can't ask…' Tom managed, but he was cut off.

'You have no choice.' Once again he heard anger, but she was moving on. 'Okay, Kit, let's get your hand fixed up ready for your helicopter ride. Dr Lavery, I'll need your help to stabilise things, but then you need to go home and pack.'

'You've only just arrived,' Tom said. He was feeling as if the ground beneath him was no longer solid. Who was in charge here? Not him. 'You can't...'

'Dr Lavery, I have no idea yet of what *you* can and can't do,' she said with asperity. 'But *me*... Don't tell *me* what I can and can't do without seeing me in operation. Do you or do you not need a childminder to stay with Rose?'

'I... Yes.'

'And is Rose dependable?'

'Of course.'

'So if I turned out to be a terrible person... would she kick me out?'

'She would,' Roscoe said from behind them. He was starting to smile—problem solved? 'If she was worried I dare say she'd boss me and Lizzy to move, with or without our new baby. She's one strong lady.'

'And so am I,' Rachel retorted. 'So, Dr Lavery, if you don't want me to stay with your boys then say so, but don't tell me I'm not capable.'

'I guess... I'm starting to think you're very capable,' Tom told her and tried to smile.

'Thank you,' Rachel told him, but there was no hint of a smile in return. He was still hearing anger. 'Now, Kit, let's get this hand fixed and show your stepdad I'm capable there as well.'

What had she promised?
*Argh!*
If there was one thing Rachel Tilding had learned in her twenty-eight years it was not to get involved.

Eight years ago she'd applied for the Roger Lavery Scholarship because it was the only one which offered to pay her entire way through medical school. Her education was sketchy, to say the least. She'd officially left school at fifteen. Since then she'd worked where she could, odds and sods for years, before ending up on night shift in a metal fabrication factory. She'd couch-surfed with anyone who'd put up with her, all the time saving, doing whatever she could to get the marks and the money to enter medical school. The day she'd heard she'd won the scholarship she'd been so tired she'd wept over the assembly line all night.

But then, thanks to the scholarship, things had eased. She'd been able to find somewhere permanent to live. She'd had security and a future, which was more than she'd ever dreamed of. The only cost to her was a contract at the end of her internship to work for two years in this end-of-the-earth place.

'Two years?' She thought of one of the other students on her med course, of his appalled re-action when she'd told him her plans. 'Shallow Bay? A tin-pot hospital with no specialists, in the middle of the National Park, cut off by bush-fires in summer, floods in winter? I'm guessing you'll be married with babies by the end of the two years because there'll be nothing else to do.'

'I'm not into families.' She'd snapped it before she could stop herself, almost a fear response.

'You will be if you go there,' her fellow stu-dent had said. 'My uncle's a county doctor, on call twenty-four-seven. His wife and kids hardly see him, but he says they're the only thing that keeps him sane.'

A family? Keeping her sane? As if.

And now she'd offered to be part of one.

But it was only for a couple of days. She could do this. After what she'd been through, she knew she could pretty much do anything she needed.

But this was what someone else needed. Tom.

A stepfather. A man who'd left his kids with someone totally irresponsible.

So why had she made the offer? It wasn't her fault the kid had hurt his hand. She didn't get involved—she never had. And yet here she was, two minutes after arriving at Shallow Bay, putting her hand up to move in with a house full of kids. It was so unlike her it left her stunned.

Was it the thought of kids being left with a stepfather? After all this time, the word still made her feel sick to the stomach.

She was overreacting, she knew she was. Cinderella's stepmother... Her own stepfather... They'd given the roles such a bad name.

One was a fairy story, she told herself, but her own...

Get over it.

Luckily she had medicine to distract her. It was a relief to move back into treating doctor mode. She was using local anaesthetic. Kit was awake and terrified, so she needed Tom to be Kit's support person.

Roscoe had set up a screen so Kit couldn't see her work. Tom could see over the screen but she had to block both Tom and Kit out. It was only Kit's hand that mattered.

The anaesthetic block was cutting off sensation and Tom was keeping the little boy still. Conscious all the time of doing no more damage, she started removing slivers of glass. Left in situ, they could move during the flight and cause more damage.

There was enough damage already. He must have dragged his hand backward as he'd felt it cut. The glass had sliced from palm down to wrist and then across as he'd jerked back out of the shattered window.

She was focusing fiercely. Broken glass was appallingly difficult to clear from wounds, as its transparency made it notoriously hard to see. Roscoe was in the background, handing her what she needed, but Tom was right there. One of his hands was under Kit's head, cradling like a pillow. The other was on Kit's elbow, stopping it moving.

Despite her concentration on the wound, she couldn't quite block out his presence. He was holding the little boy still but hugging him at the same time.

'This is going to be an amazing scar,' he was telling Kit. 'You'll need to make up a great story to go with it. Maybe we could get Dr Tilding to make marks that look like crocodile teeth to go with it. Then we could tell everyone that instead of staying with your grandparents last year you went croc hunting. Maybe one attacked Henry and you fought it off with your bare hands. I think it was a whopper, twenty feet long with teeth the size of my hedge-cutters. But you fought and fought and finally it held up its hands—paws?—what do crocodiles have? Anyway, your crocodile surrendered. And you told him it'd be okay as long as he said sorry and let you have a ride on his back.'

And to Rachel's astonishment the little boy managed a weak chuckle. 'That's silly,' he quavered. 'Kids don't ride crocodiles.'

'I bet superheroes do,' Tom said. 'This scar looks like a superhero scar. Does it look like a superhero scar to you, Dr Tilding?'

She'd just fielded a sliver of glass. She held it still for a moment in her forceps, making sure her grip was secure before she tried to shift it, then transferred it to the kidney dish.

'It'll definitely be a superhero scar,' she agreed. 'You might need to buy a new T-shirt, Kit. One with Batman on the front?'

'Batman?' Kit said, with a brief return of spirit.

With scorn to match. 'Batman's old.' And then his face crumpled as he recalled another grief. 'My meerkat T-shirt… It's all bloody.'

'We'll try and fix it,' Tom told him, but even Rachel could hear the doubt. And Roscoe grimaced behind him. To get monitors on the little boy's chest they'd simply sliced the T-shirt away, not only to get fast access but also to check there were no other lacerations underneath. The T-shirt was now a mangled mess.

But she could fix this. Rachel's splinter skill was internet shopping. Or, to be truthful, internet window-shopping—years of dreaming of what other kids could buy.

There'd been a great library in her neighbourhood and the librarian had been kind. She hadn't seemed to notice just how much time Rachel spent there—or that when her books got too much for her she'd just sort of sidled to one of the computers. Patrons were supposed to pay for fifteen-minute slots, but when the library was quiet…well, Maureen was a librarian with a kind heart and she didn't seem to notice. Sometimes Rachel had been asleep in a cubicle. Sometimes she'd been at the computer, dreaming of stuff she could never buy.

But she could buy stuff now, and memories of a weird search came back to her at just the right moment.

'Hey, I have a solution,' she told Kit. She was almost done. There'd still be tiny slivers in the wound but it would be up to the plastic surgeon in Sydney to retrieve them. The shards that could have done more damage were gone, and if she foraged more she risked making that damage worse.

'A solution?' Tom said.

'A meerkat superhero.'

'There's no such thing.'

'Of course there is. Kit, you tell him.'

'I haven't seen…' Kit said doubtfully.

'You haven't? You're obviously looking in the wrong places.'

Meerkats had been a bit of a thing for her during her teens; they had fascinated her, taken her out of her bleak world for a while. She still had a sneaky affection for them, and even now her internet browser seemed to find them almost by itself.

'You must know there are online comics,' she said. 'I bet there are even online movies and I definitely know there are meerkat superhero T-shirts. I could order you one this very night, if you want. It'll need to come from overseas so you might need to wait for a few weeks, but something like that would be worth waiting for, don't you think?'

'A meerkat superhero…?'

'Marvel the Meerkat?' she mused. 'I'm thinking that's who I saw. Maybe I have the name wrong. We'll have to wait and see.'

'But I broke your window,' Kit quavered, sounding astounded.

'So you did. So you'll have to pay.' She was closing, with steristrips because stitching a hand that needed further surgery was pointless. She glanced at Tom and saw the look of strain on his face. More than strain. She'd seen this reaction before, during her internship in an emergency department in Sydney. It was the reaction of parents whose foundations had been shaken after injury to their kids.

The look set back her prejudices a little. He cared?

So what was with the neglect? If he was a stepdad, where was Mum?

It wasn't her business. Focus on Kit. She'd just told him he'd have to pay.

'Can you fish?' she asked the little boy, guessing what the answer would be. She'd already noticed fishing rods stacked outside the next-door garage.

'Tom showed us how,' Kit said, confused.

'There you are then,' she said decisively. 'I can't catch fish but I love eating them. When your hand's better I demand three fish for payment. What's your favourite fish to catch?'

'Whiting,' Kit said and then looked doubtfully at Tom. 'Tom would have to help me.'

'I don't mind who helps,' she said. 'But I'm charging three fresh fish for my damaged window. Not all at once because I can only eat one at a time and I like them fresh. Then I'll charge two more for the new meerkat T-shirt I'll order tonight. Is that a deal?'

'D-deal,' Kit said and even managed a watery smile.

'That's that, then,' she said matter-of-factly. 'Now, if you'll excuse me, I need to unpack a few more boxes before I'm needed again.'

And she smiled at Kit, at Roscoe, but not at Tom, and then she headed out of the door.

He caught her just as she reached her car.

Her car... He saw her stop in dismay as she

saw the mess, as she realised just what damage had been done. He saw her face go blank, almost as if she'd been slapped.

Back in his office he had a file on this woman. The file was in his possession not because she was a future colleague; he had it because Rachel Tilding was the recipient of the scholarship his grandfather had endowed, and as Roger Lavery's grandson he was one of the trustees of that endowment. Every two years a scholarship was awarded to a student who wouldn't otherwise be able to attend medical school but had shown determination and rigour to get where they were.

Rachel had won the scholarship eight years ago, when Tom's father still headed the trustees, but his parents were now living overseas and the file was in Tom's possession. When it was time for Rachel to take up her appointment, Tom had hauled it out and read it.

It didn't make pretty reading. Poverty, foster homes, eventual homelessness but, throughout it all, a grinding determination to be a doctor. She hadn't had the highest marks of the applicants but her sheer grit had made the award a no-brainer.

Now she was looking at her car as if this was

a catastrophe. He watched her face crumple, her hand go to her eyes.

'Rachel?'

She gasped and swivelled, swiping her face fiercely with the back of her hand. Her long-sleeved shirt was still blood-stained where Kit had leaned on her shoulder in the car. Her soft brown curls were tangled back behind her ears, there was a smudge of blood on her cheek and her brown eyes looked too big in her too-pale face. She looked younger than the twenty-eight years she was, he thought. Defenceless? It was a strange adjective to describe her but that was how he saw her.

'You shouldn't be here,' she said, struggling to find control. 'Go back to Kit.'

'We're not really at the end of the earth,' he said gently, because something told him what was before her was more important than a messy car. 'We might not have plastic surgeons but we do have a car dealership. Roy's talent—aside from selling people cars they haven't realised they need—is detailing. He can take a farm bomb that's been lived in by farmers, pigs, dogs, whatever, and turn it into a gleaming bargain of the century. And this…'

He looked at the gorgeous scarlet lacquer, the sheer beauty of the little roadster. 'This would be his absolute pleasure to clean. The only thing you need to fear is him putting it into his showroom window when he's done.'

'Really?' She sniffed and eyed him with distrust. 'But it's blood. Don't people have rules about contamination?'

'He might charge more,' Tom agreed. 'But this was an accident, Rachel, caused by my stepson. My insurance will more than cover it.' He wasn't actually sure that it would, but there was no way he was saying that now. The responsibility was his. He'd pay a king's ransom to get her a clean car if necessary. 'Meanwhile, I'm heading to Sydney, thanks to you, so you can use my car.' He motioned to the car park, to a large serviceable SUV. 'You might even think about buying such a car for here. It's much more sensible.'

She had herself under control again now. He saw her regroup, and then gaze at his battered SUV with dislike.

'I might need to be a country doctor for two years,' she said. 'But there is nothing on earth that'd persuade me to swap my Petal for that… that…'

'Don't say it,' he said urgently, and smiled. 'That's Moby Dick, christened by the boys, and Moby's sensitive.'

'Moby doesn't look like he has a sensitive nerve in his body.'

'Looks are deceptive.' He hesitated. 'But…you will drive it? Just until I get back? Rachel, I can't tell you…'

'I don't want you to tell me,' she said, the anger he'd sensed from the start resurfacing. 'We all do what we have to do, Dr Lavery, and if that involves me driving Moby Dick…'

'And taking responsibility for two small boys. And starting work three days early. It's a huge ask.'

'It's not an ask. It's just what is,' she said. 'Whatever *what is* needs to be faced, and there's no use arguing. And for you… *What is* includes doing what you need to do for your stepsons. You've failed in that department already today so it's time to do better.'

Her anger was right there, in his face. Her brown eyes were flashing. Challenging.

'You're judging me?' he demanded.

'Of course I am. You really think Christine is a reliable childminder?'

'I had no choice.'

'Isn't keeping kids safe the most important choice of all?' She closed her eyes for a moment and seemed to collect herself. 'That's your business, however. I don't know your circumstances. It's not serious enough to report to the authorities...'

'The authorities,' he said, gobsmacked. 'You'd go there?'

'If I think children are seriously neglected, of course,' she snapped. 'Stepfather or not.'

'Is this your background speaking?'

That silenced her. She stared at him blankly for a moment before responding. 'What...what do you know of my background?'

'I'm the grandson of Roger Lavery. I'm a trustee for his scholarship fund. I read your application.'

'Then forget it,' she snapped, the picture of outrage. 'As my colleague, it smacks of prying, and it has no bearing on what's happening now. Dr Lavery, I have to organise myself if I'm to stay with your boys and so do you. The evac chopper should be here soon. You have packing to do, plus explaining to Henry and Marcus what's happening. They're confused and upset and they're still with the appalling Christine. So that's your *what is*. They need to be reassured, Christine needs to be sacked and you need to get packed. Go do it, Dr Lavery. Ring Rose if you can, and tell her I'll be there with my toothbrush in an hour.'

'Rachel, I can't tell you…'

'Then don't tell me,' she said angrily. 'And don't you dare pry into my private business again. Just get things done.'

An hour later he was sitting in the rear of the evac chopper, wondering what on earth had happened.

How had it come to this?

Kit was asleep, courtesy of the strong painkillers he'd been given. The two paramedics on board were more than capable of taking care of Kit medically. Tom's role was that of parent.

*Parent.*

The word still hung heavy.

He remembered the night Claire had asked him. 'Please, Tom, will you marry me? I can't think what else to do.'

What followed had been one marriage, three adoptions and Claire's death, and his life had changed for ever. He sat in the helicopter looking down at one injured child, thinking he'd just dumped two others on a woman he hardly knew. This was a nightmare. And if Claire's parents found out...

He raked his fingers through his hair, struggling to get his head around the logistics of this mess, and the paramedic next to him glanced at him in sympathy.

'You've had a shock too, mate. We can set you up on the other stretcher if you like, give you a chance to close your eyes and regroup.'

It needed only this, to be treated as a patient.

But that was what he felt like at the moment, as if he'd been punched in the guts. He was so out of his depth.

Who was the woman in charge of his children? A fiery newcomer who'd judged him and found him wanting. A woman he'd met only hours before.

He had Roscoe in the background, he reminded himself, and he had Rose. They'd keep an eye on her.

But her anger stayed with him.

He looked down at Kit's white face, at his limp little body. These kids had been through so much. And his lack of care had caused more pain… She'd been right to look at him with fury.

'Lie down,' the paramedic said again, gently, and he thought maybe he needed to.

He looked sick because that was how he felt.

What had she done, offering to mind two boys for days?

She didn't get involved. Ever. What crazy impulse had led her to say she'd help out?

Medicine was what Rachel used to settle her and it was medicine she focused on now. She sat in Tom's office and read through histories of the patients in the hospital. Five were elderly, recuperating from falls or waiting for home care arrangements. Three were here for rehab, transferred back from city hospitals, preparing to go home. One was a thirty-seven-weeks-pregnant mum with five kids at home. Tom had written in heavy letters—*'Bed rest until her sister arrives from Canada!'*

The final history was that of a farmer with an infected leg after being kicked by a cow. According to the history, he was responding to antibiotics. There seemed nothing she couldn't handle.

She did a round and introduced herself. Without exception, the patients were full of questions but she backed away fast. That was something else she'd been warned of with country medicine. 'Everyone will know everything about you in two minutes.'

Tom Lavery already knew more about her than she was comfortable with. At least she could back away from patients before they got personal.

Roscoe found her as she saw the last one. 'Everything's arranged,' he told her. 'Christine's feeling bad about what's happened. Big of her, but she's decided to be helpful. She's moving her Aunt Rose in now. Rose will give everyone the hugs they need. The boys love her. If you can...your job is just to be there at the edges. Make sure Rose doesn't start washing or scrubbing. She has osteoarthritis and her hip's probably more painful than she's letting on, but she loves the boys.'

'That's great,' Rachel said, feeling relieved. 'I can do whatever else needs to be done but the hugging is her department.'

She didn't do hugging. Almost unconsciously, her fingers drifted to one of the bands of scar tissue she could still feel around her upper arms.

After twenty-eight years she didn't know how to hug. She didn't know how to love, and she had no intention of trying.

So now what?

'Roy Matheson's outside, checking the damage to your car,' Roscoe told her. 'Tom must have phoned him. All he needs is your keys and he reckons he'll have her good as new in no time. Here are Doc's keys for Moby Dick. We'll call you back if we need you. Meanwhile, you go and do what you have to do.' He hesitated. 'You know how grateful we all are that you're doing this? It's really generous.'

'I hardly had a choice.' She couldn't help it; her voice sounded waspish.

'You could have refused. We'd have found a way. This is a tight community. If you hadn't offered we'd have muddled through somehow. No one's left in the lurch here. We care.'

And why did that make her feel weird?

Her childhood. The loneliness.

*No one's left in the lurch here.*

Enough. She gave herself a mental shake and took the proffered car keys. She needed to find... Moby Dick? She also needed to figure out the boundaries of the next few days.

For boundaries had to be set, she told herself. Boundaries were what she lived within.

She could do this.

But at the back of her mind a question was niggling. She'd wanted to ask Roscoe but her boundaries had stopped her.

These were Tom's stepsons—what on earth was a man doing with three kids who weren't his own?

Hadn't he heard of boundaries?

# CHAPTER THREE

THREE DAYS LATER the medevac chopper deposited Tom and a recuperating Kit back home, on the landing pad three hundred metres from Shallow Bay Hospital.

They'd arrived earlier than Tom had expected. Air transfer was available only in emergencies. Transfer home to Shallow Bay wasn't classified as an emergency. That meant Tom had been trying to decide whether to hire a car or wait for road ambulance transfer. However, on Monday morning a scuba diver had come up too fast after a dive south of Shallow Bay. Worse, he'd gone diving alone. He was in extremis when his friends found him and he'd died before they'd found somewhere with enough mobile coverage to ring emergency services.

The coroner needed the body and the coroner was in Sydney. Thus the chopper was on its way, but there was no rush. The crew who'd taken Tom and Kit to Sydney had kept tabs on where

Kit's treatment was up to. Kit's hand was stable, with no more need for specialist intervention. They'd been offered a ride back.

Thus they rode back in style, arriving at Shallow Bay mid-morning. Tom emerged from the chopper and lifted Kit down after him. A still shaky Kit stood by his side until Roscoe drove up to meet them.

'Hey!' he boomed in greeting, and Tom was aware of a wash of relief at the sight of his friend's broad smile, at the hug Roscoe was giving Kit. 'It's great to see you, mate,' he told Kit and then he straightened and grinned at Tom. 'And you too.' Tom's hand was enveloped; the hold was tantamount to a hug, and Tom felt better for it. 'It's great to have you back.'

'The place hasn't fallen apart without us?' Tom took Kit's good hand and held on because the little boy was still shaky. His arm was a swathe of white under his sling but it wasn't only the shock and the injury that was making him shaky, Tom thought. These kids had had their foundations shaken by their mother's death.

'All good,' Roscoe was saying. 'You've hardly been missed. Our Dr Rachel is a beauty.'

'Really?'

'Efficiency R Us,' Roscoe said. 'You have no idea how a ward round should be conducted until you see Our Rachel at work. She can get a full history in less than three minutes. The patients don't know what's hit them.'

'You're saying she cuts corners?'

'I didn't imply that at all,' Roscoe said, swinging Kit up into his arms, giving Tom the illusion—at least for a moment—that responsibility was shared. 'No corner dares to be cut on Dr Rachel's watch. Now, mate,' he said to Kit, 'where are you up to?'

'We'll be keeping Kit in hospital for the next few days,' Tom told him. 'Until his stitches are out.' The job the plastic surgeons had done on Kit's hand was stunning but broken stitches could see him being sent back to Sydney. There was no way he was letting Kit near his rough-and-tumble brothers until they were out.

He'd need to spend time with him, running through the exercises the hand therapist had set. At least with Rachel here he'd have the time. To have an efficient colleague was a blessing.

But what Roscoe was saying had sown doubts. He thought of the frail, elderly patients in his hospital, their need for human contact, for reassurance, and he thought, Three minutes for a history?

'Where's Rachel now?' he asked.

'On a house call,' Roscoe said. 'Herbert Daly. District nurse asked if she'll check his legs. He has three ulcers now, but the old coot won't take care of them, nor will he come in. But Rachel's on to it. Expect to see him in Ward One by lunchtime.'

'She's bossy?'

'Just organised,' Roscoe said. 'You'll see for yourself soon enough. Now, Kit, I'm betting your dad would like to take your gear home and catch up with Rose. Your brothers are both at school. How lucky are you to get this time off? Let's get you settled into the kids' ward. We have the best video games, plus Xavier Trentham's in there with a broken leg. He fell out of a tree on Saturday. He's in your class, isn't he? Dr Rachel's fixed his leg but she's keeping him in hospital until the swelling goes down and she can put a proper cast on. Meanwhile, he's aching for company. Come in and help him fight it out with Battle-Axe Warriors or whatever you kids play when we leave you alone with those game consoles. Tom will be back to see you within an hour, right, Tom?'

'Why do I feel like *I'm* being organised?' Tom said faintly and Roscoe chuckled.

'It's rubbing off,' he said. 'The Rachel effect. She's here for two years—I can't begin to imagine how we'll be by the end of it.'

'Assembly line medicine?'

'She's not that bad,' Roscoe said. 'She's good.'

But underneath Tom thought he heard doubt.

'Go see Rose and she'll tell you the same,' Roscoe said and lifted Kit into the car.

'I'll walk,' Tom said, grabbing his gear. 'It's only five minutes. It'll give me space to get my head organised.'

'See, what did I tell you?' Roscoe said and chuckled again. 'Organisation. The Rachel effect already.'

The lovely, dependable Rose was settled on the living room window seat overlooking the bay when he arrived. He paused at the door, taking in the scene before she realised he'd returned.

This place had been his grandparents' home, where he'd come for holidays as a kid. He'd loved it. He'd had freedom to wander. He'd learned to surf here. The locals had always made him welcome, had always treated him as a local.

But then his career had taken off and life had become frenetic, fun, city-centric. With his grandparents dead, his parents overseas, there'd been little reason to come back to Shallow Bay. It was only when he'd been landed with three grieving kids that he'd thought the only place they could be happy was here.

There'd been no other way. Decision made, he'd moved them here and tried to be content with the messy, kid-filled space his life had become.

But it wasn't messy now. Rose was sitting with her feet up, placidly knitting. That part felt normal. The rest of it, though, wasn't normal in the least. His usually messy house looked as if some sort of whirling dervish had swept through, but instead of creating chaos it had transformed it into… Home Beautiful?

Occasionally, during his bachelor existence, after the cleaner had been in, his city apartment had looked this tidy, but this was different. Not only was his house tidy, it seemed to have been transformed.

The furniture was arranged differently, invitingly, not wherever the kids had hauled it to get it out of the way when they were playing. Rugs were neat, vacuumed, not a wrinkle in sight. The pictures on the walls, seascapes painted by his grandmother, pictures he hadn't even realised were out of line, were now in straight lines. A couple that had descended to be propped on the floor had been rehung.

There was more. The jumble of seashells—generations of family beachcombing left in dusty piles wherever—was now arranged on a side table, with a couple of pieces of driftwood supporting them. Instead of a jumble, the shells now looked like an eye-catching art installation. The kids' books and puzzles were tidy but, more than that, they'd been arranged in enticing stacks. There was a jar of native bottlebrush on the sideboard, crimson, gorgeous.

Tuffy, the kids' fox terrier, bought in desperation from a rescue shelter in those first appalling weeks after Claire's death, had been asleep on the mat. He'd sensed Tom's arrival now and was rising to greet him. Last week Tom had been dumb enough to give him a bone and the resulting mess had still been horrible when he'd had to leave. Now he looked brushed, washed, almost presentable.

'Rachel's an amazing lady.' Rose had now realised he was there and was smiling a welcome. 'Welcome home. She hasn't let me do anything.'

'So don't do anything now,' he said. 'I'll make you a cup of tea.'

'I'd like to go home if I can,' she said, rising and packing away her knitting. 'I'll come back before the boys get home from school. Rachel and I have it organised. Tell me, how's Kit?'

He told her and her face cleared. 'Well, that's wonderful. We can go back to our old arrangement then, me being on call as needed. But Rachel tells me she's here too, if I need her. She's very bossy about my hip. I haven't felt so fussed over for years.'

'She sounds…bossy.' Tom had stooped to pat Tuffy but he was still looking around the room, still trying to figure all the differences.

'She likes to be busy,' Rose said, and he heard the same doubt he'd heard in Roscoe's voice. 'She's kind, but she can't sit still. Last night there was a lovely movie on the telly but she was polishing every shell while she watched it.'

'That's…great.'

'And cooking. She has three casseroles and two pies in the freezer for you. I told her I usually cook for you and she said, "Not with your hip."'

'I'll thank her.'

'You do that,' she said and then she paused. 'Oh, here's your car now. She must be dropping by to check on me before she goes back to the hospital. She makes me feel like I'm a patient myself.' She paused. 'Not that I'm not grateful, but I'll slip out the back way and leave you two together.' And she gathered her knitting and disappeared.

Tom Lavery was on the rug in front of the fire. He was scratching behind the ears of the misbegotten little mutt the kids called Tuffy. Tuffy was practically turning inside out with pleasure.

And for some reason the sight of this man stopped Rachel in her tracks.

She had things to do. She'd dropped by to make sure Rose was okay, and then she was due at clinic. Tom's call to Roscoe had said he'd be back some time today. She hadn't expected him this early.

He was tall, six two or maybe more. His dark brown hair was a bit unruly, tousled, sun-bleached at the ends. He was wearing casual chinos and a short-sleeved khaki shirt. His deep green eyes were crinkled at the edges—from the sun? As he looked up at her she thought he looked weary.

He'd have been at Kit's bedside for most of the last few days, she thought, remembering legions of parents watching over their kids in the paediatric wards of her training days. Some hospitals provided beds for parents, but medical imperatives and the needs of scared, ill or hurting children meant sleep was hardly ever an option.

There'd be a reason this guy looked haggard.

And maybe tiredness was a constant state for him. Roscoe had filled her in on his background over the weekend, not because she'd asked—he'd just told her.

'Tom was a surgeon in Sydney until the boys' mother died,' he'd told her. 'Their dad disappeared. Tom's all they've got.'

The boys were his stepsons. He'd married their mother and then she'd died, Roscoe had told her.

But how could he care so much for kids who weren't his? It was beyond her but looking at him now she had no doubt that he did care, and he was exhausted because of it.

Roscoe's story had made her feel more than a little guilty that she'd let her prejudice show when she'd first met him. He might be a step-dad, but stepfathers shouldn't all be tarred by the same brush. It was just the word. *Stepfather*... After all these years it still made her feel ill.

'Welcome home,' she said now, trying for a smile. His obvious weariness seemed to be making something twist inside her. Normal sympathy for a tired and worried parent? For some reason it felt more than that, and the sensation made her unsettled.

'How's Kit?' she asked, pushing aside her niggle of unease, heading back to talk medicine. Work was always safest.

'Roscoe's putting him into a bed in the kids' ward,' he told her. 'The surgery's gone well. Flexor tendons were damaged as well as nerves but the surgeon's done a great job and he has every hope that there'll be no long-term damage. If he was an only child I'd bring him home, but he and his brothers play rough. He has a protective plaster so maybe I'm being ultra-cautious, but given how far we are from help I'd prefer him to stay where he is until the stitches are out. He knows I'll be in and out. Henry and Marcus can visit. It's good to have him home.'

Then he gazed around the room again, slowly, as if taking it in. 'It's good to be home too,' he said. 'Thank you for your care.'

She followed his gaze, noting with satisfaction that nothing had been disturbed after her clean. 'You're welcome. I'm not bad at dusting and polishing.'

'It's not actually the dusting and polishing I'm thanking you for,' he told her with a slightly crooked smile. 'That's great, but with three kids I've pretty much learned not to value them. It's for starting at the hospital three days early, but mostly it's for caring for Marcus and Henry— and for Rose too. I can't tell you how grateful I am.'

'It's just what needed to be done.' She shifted uncomfortably. He was thanking her for care rather than cooking and cleaning? She didn't care, at least not in the emotional sense. She did what she had to do to keep her world functioning as it should, to keep her patients safe, to keep herself safe. She accepted responsibility when she had to, but that was as far as it went.

Caring was something that had been driven

out of her from a time so long ago she could scarcely remember.

So now…she looked at Tom's weary smile, seeing the telltale lines of strain around his eyes, and she thought it wasn't caring to accept a little more responsibility. It was simply doing what needed to be done.

'You look like you could do with a sleep,' she told him. 'Why don't you take a nap now? Roscoe and I have things covered. There's nothing urgent. We don't need you.'

'I'd like to see everyone, though,' he said diffidently. 'You've been out to see Herbert Daly?'

'His son's bringing him into hospital,' she told him. 'He should have been in days ago, but he's stubborn. I had to insist.'

'He likes his own space,' Tom said neutrally. 'But you're right—he could do with some bed rest. What about the rest of our patients?'

'Frances Ludeman's still in. Her blood pressure's still up but only mildly. It was only after her husband brought the other *five* kids in to visit that I saw why you wanted her to stay.'

'She needs all the rest she can get,' Tom said. 'And Roscoe says Xavier Trentham's in the kids' ward.'

'Fractured tibia. It's a clean break but he fell through a hedge and there's too much swelling to cast it yet. Like your Kit, there's too much chaos at home for him to be safe without the cast.'

'Chaos?'

'Other kids.'

'Right.' He gave her an odd, sideways it looked like she didn't understand. It felt strange, doing what seemed like a medical handover in his living room, but efficiency seemed to be called for. He moved on. 'Bob's infection from the cow kick?'

'There's still some necrosis. He wants to go home but I've said another three days.'

'He'll hate another three days. We can probably organise him to go home with visits from district nursing.'

'He'll need more than just nursing. He'll need to be checked, by you or by me.'

'I can do that.'

'Why? It's much easier to keep him in hospital.'

'Yes, but he has problems,' he told her. 'Have you met his wife?'

'I gave Lois an update yesterday. She's accepted that he won't be home until Thursday at soonest. He has no choice.'

'He does have a choice. I'll organise it.'

'Why?' she asked, startled. 'You can hardly do house calls. He lives fifteen minutes out of town.'

'I don't mind. Lois's stressed herself. She has high blood pressure, and she worries about a daughter living in New Zealand. I suspect they care for her financially and that's pushing the farm income. I don't want Lois ill.'

'But it's Bob who's your patient.'

'I need to care for them all,' he said simply. 'Like I need to go do a ward round now.'

She stilled. 'I've already done a round. You don't trust that I've looked after them?'

'I'm not saying that.' He was watching her as if he was trying to understand something that was puzzling him. 'Rachel, this is a country medical practice. We don't treat patients in isolation. Every person comes with a story around them, farms that need tending, debts, kid worries, elderly parent concerns. If you ignore them then they come back to bite you. This is your first shot at family medicine, right?'

'Yes.'

'And you're only doing it because of the scholarship?'

'I'm hugely grateful for the scholarship,' she said, a bit awkwardly.

'But family medicine isn't what you want long-term?'

'I'm pushing for radiology.'

'Where you don't need to look much past the image to the patient.'

'Is that a criticism?'

'Of course it's not.' He shrugged, and once again she had the impression of deep weariness. 'Heaven knows we need good radiologists—they helped save Kit's hand. But here it's purely country practice, and country practice means looking out for everyone. If we leave Bob in hospital for much longer, Lois's blood pressure will go through the roof. We send him home.'

His tone was final. Fair enough, she conceded. Tom was, after all, the senior doctor in this set-up. But to choose to do house calls when there was an alternative... She'd had to do a couple already and they made her uneasy. It felt like stepping into an intimate space she had no right to enter.

'I'll do the house calls,' he told her. 'If they worry you.'

How had he guessed? Was her face so transparent?

'We share the work,' she told him brusquely. 'My contract says full-time family practice for two years. I can do it.'

'You'll be a better radiologist for time spent in family medicine,' he said, still with that odd assessing look on his face. 'Believe it or not, I believe I'm becoming a better doctor because of it. And I can still do some surgery, which is my passion.'

'You're joking. How much surgery can you perform here?'

'Not as much as I'd like,' he admitted. 'But I do the small stuff. Ferndale has specialists, but it's a hard drive, all curves and kangaroos. Cath Harrison's the anaesthetist there. She comes over to Shallow Bay once a week or so, and we do a list together. Simple stuff that would be a pain for the locals to have to go to Ferndale—or Sydney—to get done. It keeps me happy.'

'But it's simple surgery.' How on earth could it make him content? 'So how can you say you're a better doctor because of what you're doing here?'

'Because I'm learning to treat the whole patient,' he told her. 'I hope you can get what that means. But now... I'll head over to do a ward round and then get to clinic.'

'I'm running the clinic and there's no necessity to do a ward round. I told you. Everyone's sorted.'

'So Roscoe said.' Once again she got that wash of weariness. This man should be in bed, but he wasn't going there. 'I need to see everyone...for me,' he admitted. 'I'm not doubting your medicine.'

'Then why aren't you being sensible?' She knew she was sounding stubborn, but so was he.

He took a deep breath, regrouping. 'Okay,' he conceded. 'You take clinic, as long as you ring me for any problems, but I will do a ward round.'

'You don't trust me.'

'I do trust you. Your credentials are impeccable.'

'Then what?'

'Rachel, it's just because I care for them as people,' he said, sounding a bit helpless. 'I need to see for myself how everyone's doing, and it's not just the medical side I'm interested in.'

'I don't know what you mean.'

'Which is why you're here for two years and I'm stuck here for life,' he said, and suddenly his voice was grim. 'As doctors... Rachel, you and I might have belonged to the same species once upon a time, but now... Well, somehow, I've evolved into a different breed. Darwin might have said I've evolved through necessity, for survival. Your survival's assured. You're just marking time before you can head back to your own world. But here, Dr Tilding, I need you to pretend to evolve, just for two years. You're useless here without caring.'

Then he shook his head. 'I'm sorry. That's probably too big a statement. You obviously do care. You're responsible and you're generous and I'm deeply grateful. Believe me, I'm grateful for what you've already done. Anything else has to be an extra.'

They walked back to the hospital together, but they walked in silence. He'd offended her, Tom thought. He knew what he'd said had been clumsy, but he was too tired to get the nuances right.

So now she walked beside him and he couldn't think where to take it. And it wasn't just tiredness that was throwing him. Would he have accused any other doctor of not caring? After she'd spent the last three days doing just that, it seemed unfair.

There was something about her that had him off balance.

She was gorgeous. Half a head smaller than he was, she was packaged just right. Bouncy brown curls—well, he'd seen them bouncy, though she had them tied up tight now. Brown eyes, nicely spaced. A wide, generous mouth and a smattering of freckles. She was dressed conservatively—too conservatively for such a warm day, in neat black trousers and a long-sleeved shirt—but her plain clothes didn't disguise the curves underneath.

It wasn't the fact that she was cute—well, more than cute—that had him off balance, but he didn't know why.

Was it the bleak notes in her scholarship application? Was it the way she'd said the word *stepfather*, as if the name itself conjured horror? Was it the anger he'd seen when she'd thought the boys were neglected?

Or was it the traces of fear that appeared and

disappeared, as if there were things, emotions, Rachel Tilding was still hiding?

How did you get over a childhood of neglect?

Tom had had a blessed childhood. His father had left Shallow Bay early—*'I can't stand the sight of blood—there's no way I could have done medicine.'* He'd done law, been hugely successful, moved into politics and then into international diplomacy. His mother's career was equally impressive. Tom's arrival had been an accident—they'd been too busy to have children—but in the end they'd welcomed him. They were a power couple but their love for their only son had been unstinting.

As his grandparents' love had been. Tom had had the run of embassies, of political powerhouses, and of Shallow Bay. He'd learned languages, he'd studied, he'd surfed, he'd dated gorgeous women, he'd had fun.

He'd also rescued things. Anything. Beetles lying upside down on wet paths. Unwanted kittens. Bullied kids at school.

He couldn't bear to see hurt, even though sometimes caring caused chaos.

Like the time he'd brought a huntsman spider home, a female, laden with a huge egg sac.

He'd found it at the back of the lockers at school, missing two legs, and decided to rehome it in the laundry. He'd forgotten to tell his mother—who'd found about a thousand baby spiders in her clean washing.

Like the first time he'd seen Claire, being yelled at by her father as she was dropped off at infant school.

Like the time Claire had phoned him after her diagnosis. 'Please, Tom, help me...'

Was the same drive to fix things attracting him to Rachel? He'd always been a sucker for the needy. He knew it.

'It's just the way you're made,' he told himself. 'It's in your DNA. So leave it. Rachel doesn't need you. She's tough and she's bright and she'll do what it takes to get on in life. You do the same.'

It made sound sense.

So why did a niggle of doubt tell him that life was about to get more complicated?

# CHAPTER FOUR

THE WEEK THAT followed was busy but not frantic—thanks to Rachel. Her efficiency might set some patients' backs up, it might make Tom edgy, but there was no doubting that it lowered his workload.

Heather Lewis, breeder of Hereford cattle, president of the local Country Women's Association and stander of no nonsense, met him in the car park late on Friday. He'd just returned from a house call. Heather sauntered over to meet him, a big woman, bluff, kind, bossy. Ready to gossip.

'She's good, isn't she?' she said without preamble.

'You mean Rachel?'

'I've just been to see her for my foot. Fungal infection. She gave me a script, instructions and a lecture about wearing wet boots. In and out in five minutes. That's my kind of medicine.'

'Hmm,' he said doubtfully. It was the kind of medicine Heather liked, and mostly it was what people needed, but how many consultations were that easy?

'And she's here for two years. We need to get her involved. Does she play tennis? Ride a horse? Play mah-jong? I tried asking but she brushed me off. Fair enough, it was a medical consult after all. But what's she interested in, Tom? How can we pull her into the community?'

'I have no idea,' he said faintly. 'She seems to like keeping herself to herself.'

'But she's there when you need her. It was trial by fire, landing her with your boys last week. She must be a good'un. Worth prodding below the surface.'

'I guess.'

'And she's single,' Heather went on relentlessly. 'There's a thought, Doc. You and her… You could surely use help with those boys. You still got Kit in hospital?'

'He'll be home tomorrow.'

'They're a handful. A partner would be good. You might want to think about it.' And Heather drove away and left him standing.

Think about what?

Rachel?

A love life?

Ha.

Even if he had the time for such things—which he didn't—even if there was a possibility of dating when he was solely responsible for the care of three troubled kids… *Rachel?* An uptight, self-contained woman who'd stepped in when needed but who'd stepped away fast.

As any woman would from his situation.

But the niggle he'd felt almost a week ago was growing, and as he walked back into the hospital he allowed himself a moment to think about it. Rachel Tilding was about as far from his type of woman as it was possible to get. BK—Before Kids—he'd had a definite kind of partner. Not serious—never serious. He liked feisty, fun women who didn't take life too seriously. Women who could give as much as they got, who demanded no promises, who didn't cling, who were happy to step into his world and then out again as life called them in a different direction.

There didn't seem a lot of joy in Rachel Tilding's world. Life seemed serious. Organised.

He put the idea firmly aside, heading in to walk through the wards and say hi to everyone who'd appreciate a visit. There wasn't much for him to do medically. Rachel had obviously done her rounds earlier. Charts had been filled in. Every need had been met.

Except talking. He talked his way round the hospital now, calming worries, explaining, listening. Just being there.

His final visit for the day was Kit. Tom had been in a few times during the day, as much as he could manage. Now he found him engrossed in a battleship conflict. His friend, Xavier, was still in the next bed. There'd been no pressure on the ward, so the decision had been made to keep them longer. They were both due to go home in the morning.

Tom got a short greeting between battles—plus a quick, one-armed hug which was a message on its own. Kit might be content for the moment, but he was still needy.

Finally he headed home. From the track he could see Rose in her favourite seat. She'd be knitting while the kids watched the telly show they always watched on Friday nights. He'd go in, say goodnight to Rose and then cook his standard Friday night fare of hamburgers.

And try not to miss Friday nights of the past. Socialising. Fun.

Suddenly he was hesitating. Rachel's arrival

really had made a difference. It was only five-thirty, far earlier than he usually finished. The ingredients for hamburgers were in the fridge and Rose would enjoy putting them together. She liked eating with the boys. It was a warm night. The beach beckoned.

He could use some me time.

Ten minutes later he'd headed back to town and bought two low-alcohol beers—he was on call. A sunset, a beer, time to reflect—it wasn't up to the standard of Friday nights of his past, but it'd have to do.

He parked outside his cottage. Rose saw him from the window. He waved towards the beach, put his finger to his mouth in a signal for her not to tell the boys, and she waved back her acknowledgement.

Bless her, he thought. She'd guess he needed space. What would he do without her?

Life was okay, he told himself as he walked down the beach path. He had a great housekeeper. He had a colleague to share his work, to halve his call roster.

He had two low-alcohol stubbies to celebrate Friday night.

Alone.

'Morose R Us,' he muttered as he headed down the track. 'Get over it.' There wasn't a thing he could do about his situation and self-pity would get him nowhere. He needed to be grateful that Kit was okay, that Rose was giving him space, that he had two stubbies—and he had a new colleague.

He rounded the bend that blocked the view of the bay from the track—and his new colleague was sitting on the sand in front of him.

She'd obviously been swimming. Her hair, normally tied tightly back, had come loose and was coiling wetly down her bare back. She was wearing a simple one-piece bathing suit. She looked…

Gorgeous?

She swivelled and struggled to her feet, grabbing her towel to cover herself—and all he could see was fear.

She hauled the towel up in front of her.

Not fast enough.

Every time he'd seen this woman she'd been wearing long sleeves. At work she wore formal business-type blouses, tucked into trousers or skirts. At home she wore long-sleeved T-shirts with jeans or shorts.

He thought of the first time he'd seen her, with Kit. She'd been wearing a long-sleeved shirt then. It had been covered with blood and looked truly shocking.

What he saw now, in the moment before she hauled the towel around her, seemed just as shocking.

Blotches were etched deep into the skin of her upper arms. No, not blotches. Scars. Many scars. He hardly had time to see them though, before the towel was wrapped around her, shutting them from view.

She was standing now, fear fading as she realised who he was. But she took a step back, making a clear delineation between the two of them.

'Sorry,' she muttered, her voice shaky. 'I shouldn't have sat so close to the path.'

'And I should have whistled as I walked,' he told her, trying to drive away the panic he still sensed. 'I usually do. It scares the Joe Blakes.'

'Joe Blakes?'

'What the locals call snakes. The advice is to sing as you walk, but if you heard me sing you'd know that it'd scare more than Joe Blakes.'

'Are there snakes here?' Her voice was still

shaky but he knew it wasn't from fear of snakes. Why was she frightened?

'I doubt it,' he told her, gentling his voice. 'It pays to be careful, but we haven't seen any in the dunes for ages. They're more scared of us than we are of them. The boys' noise will be keeping them at bay.'

'Oh,' she said neutrally, and he could see her fight to get her face under control. Her towel was drawn tight, concealing all.

Or not quite. One of the scars was just above her breast. Until now he'd put her long sleeved tops and high necklines down to her general uptightness. Now...

He'd seen scars like this. A long time ago. In paediatric ward during his training.

Abuse.

Cigarette burns.

*Hell.*

'Rachel...'

'I was just going,' she stammered, reaching down for her bag. 'I came down for a swim after work, to get some peace. I imagine that's what you want, too. I'll leave you to it.'

She was ready to bolt.

*Cigarette burns.*

He knew nothing about this woman apart from the fact that she had an impeccable medical record—and she'd won his grandfather's scholarship. And there'd been foster homes.

Her scars were completely covered now, and he couldn't ask. Maybe she hoped he hadn't seen them.

He had to leave it like that, but he didn't want her to bolt. There were ghosts behind this woman's façade, and he was intrigued.

'You know, once upon a time when I finished work on Friday nights I'd head to the pub beside the hospital,' he told her, casually moving so he wasn't blocking her way. So she knew she could leave if she wanted to. 'Half the medics we worked with would be there. I can't remember a single moment of peace but I wouldn't have missed it for quids. Noise, laughter, a general debrief of the week's traumas. Friends.'

He looked down at the two stubbies he was carrying and made a decision, right there and then, that the supreme sacrifice was called for.

'So the drinks menu here might be limited,' he told her. 'But, in memory of all those Friday nights, I'm very happy to share. Do you drink beer?'

The fear and shock were subsiding. She had herself together. Almost. 'I need to go home,' she said.

'No, *I* need to go home,' he told her. 'But not yet.' Why did he get the feeling she wanted to run? He was sensing his way, the same way he'd approach a scared and wounded child. Or a startled kangaroo. 'The roster says *I'm* on call tonight, not you,' he said. 'The boys are at home, but Rose is with them and they're happy and settled. Kit's safely in hospital. My phone's in my pocket and I can be there in minutes if I'm called. I have a sliver of time to myself.'

'Which is why you need peace.'

'Which is why I need company,' he said bluntly. 'Of the adult variety. Of the colleague variety. Which is why I'm making the extraordinary gesture of offering you one of my precious stubbies.'

She stared at him for a long moment, as if trying to read his mind. Then she looked down at his stubbies.

'You brought two.'

'And I'm offering you one. You can't imagine how generous that makes me feel.'

Her lips twitched, just a little.

'Beer,' she said.

'I know, a piña colada with a sliver of lime and a wee umbrella would be more appropriate, but the ice would have melted while I walked down here. You want to slum it with me?' And before she could answer he plonked himself down on the sand.

She stood, looking down at him. Disconcerted? She was torn—he could sense it. Part of her wanted to leave, but it would have been a rebuff.

He set the stubbies in the sand and waited. Stay or go? He was aware, suddenly, that he was holding his breath. Hoping?

Why? She was simply a colleague, paying her dues for two years before she got on with her life.

Or…what? Was that a tiny sliver of hope? A resurrection of something he'd once taken for granted?

Like a love life.

Heather's words came back to him. Dumb. Ridiculous. He knew it.

Still, he kind of hoped she'd stay.

'I don't mind a beer,' she said tentatively, and he grimaced.

'Lady, you're going to have to do better than that. I carried two stubbies all the way down here. That's a fair commitment on my part. So now I'm offering to share, but not with someone who "doesn't mind a beer." It has to be "I'd love a beer" or nothing.'

And suddenly she smiled. He'd seen her smile before, greeting patients, being pleasant, but her smiles had been tight, smiles to put people at ease. This one, though, was something much more. It was a wide, white smile with a chuckle behind it.

Cute.

More than cute. Gorgeous.

'My lukewarm response was simply because you pre-empted your kind invitation with a vision of piña colada and umbrella,' she admitted and, splendidly, she sat herself down on the sand again. But where most women—most anybody—would set the towel down and sit on it, she kept it firmly wrapped around her arms, a cover for what lay beneath.

'Where in Shallow Bay would I get a piña colada?' she asked, and he had to stop thinking about scars on arms and focus on what was important. Piña coladas.

'Dougal's pub doesn't run to them, that's for sure,' he said. 'I had to twist his arm to stock low-alcohol beer. Apparently, it's for sissies.'

'Or doctors on call.'

'As you say. So…beer or no beer?'

And her smile flashed out again. 'I really would love a beer.'

That smile… He found himself grinning to match, though he wasn't actually sure what he was grinning about. She disconcerted him and he didn't understand that either.

So back to basics. He twisted the ring-pull and handed her a bottle, then did the same for himself. 'Here's to the end of your first week,' he told her, clinking bottles. 'May your next week be not so exciting.'

'Apart from the first couple of hours when your son tried to stab himself to death, it hasn't been very exciting at all,' she told him. She took a swig of her beer and seemed to enjoy it. 'I suspect it's been a lot more exciting for you, and I'm so glad it's turned out well.'

'You and me both. And I'm incredibly grateful. I wish it could have been piña colada.'

'I told you, I'd love a beer.' She held up her bottle and regarded it with affection. 'The fact that I've been on the beach for two hours and forgot my water bottle—and there's no piña colada in sight—has nothing to do with it. Beer's great.'

And there was the smile again. He liked it. A lot.

'But wouldn't you be more comfortable drinking your beer at home?' she queried, and he thought, She's made the decision to come down here—alone. It confirmed what he was learning of her. She was a woman who valued her own company, which made what she'd offered to do last weekend even more extraordinary.

'The kids are at home,' he said. 'Added to that, they have a video game which requires at least three players. It involves bombs and flames and dragon babies turning into things I don't want to think about.'

'So...' she said cautiously. 'They play it a lot?'

'Is that a judgement?'

'Hey, I'm no judge. I'm just happy to have intact windows.'

'Yeah,' he said morosely. 'You and me both. The game's okay. Fun, even. But, right now, they can't play because, stupidly, I bought a game that needs at least three players. I bought it so they'd be forced to include Henry, who often gets left out. Unfortunately, Kit's now away. Rose holds up her knitting like armour whenever they approach, so I'm their only available third man.

It's a wonder they didn't have you playing last weekend.'

'They tried,' she said. 'I was busy.'

'Is that what you said?'

'Of course.'

'Then why doesn't that statement work for me?'

'You're obviously a softie,' she told him. 'But if you don't like playing with them…'

He knew what she was asking. It was the question that he asked himself more than a dozen times a day. 'You want to know why I took them on?'

'It's none of my business,' she said hastily, and he sighed and took another swig of beer and wished he'd had the forethought to buy a dozen.

'I do like playing with them,' he admitted. 'Mostly. But that's what got me into trouble in the first place.'

'I don't get it.'

'Their mother was my best friend,' he said simply. 'We were mates from pre-school, right through med. school and beyond. Never lovers, though. Claire had appalling taste in men, from the time she kissed Terry Hopkins behind the shelter sheds when she was ten. Hopkins used to squash snails down girls' dresses. Why did she not see that could only end in tears?'

'She married a snail-squasher?'

'She escaped Terry Hopkins but she did worse. She married a serial cheat and a bully. Claire's parents are loaded. Her father's something huge in the financial world. My parents are wealthy enough, but they're nothing compared to Claire's. Steve took one look at only-child Claire's inheritance prospects and moved right in. But as soon as they were married he reverted to the slimeball he was. He had affair after affair, treating Claire like dirt.'

'Which left you as a friend.'

'I'm godfather to each of them,' he said, trying to eke out his beer to last through a bleak story. 'And they're great kids. Claire and I worked in the same hospital as interns. It was easy to help her out in emergencies. I didn't mind taking them to soccer on Saturdays, doing the occasional childminding. It was even fun.'

'Until…'

'Until.' He gave up on his stubby, planting it in the sand. It was still a quarter full but maybe he'd need it at the end.

He usually hated telling this story, but he

glanced at Rachel and saw only casual interest—the sort of interest a doctor might show a patient describing symptoms. She wasn't emotionally involved. She was simply a colleague who was...asking.

Strangely, it made it easier to keep talking. Every one of his friends had reacted to his story with dismay, horror, sympathy. Rachel was asking—because she'd like to know? Or because she thought she ought to ask. The differentiation was hard to make but somehow he appreciated it.

Her detachment made the story easier to tell.

'Claire was diagnosed with hypertrophic cardiomyopathy when Henry was two,' he told her. 'She collapsed at work. Dramatic. Awful. If she hadn't been in a hospital when it happened she would have died but she pulled through. Just. By this time Creepy Steve was almost a thing of the past and her illness was the last straw. He never had time for the kids and when Claire fell ill, when her parents made it clear there'd be no money for him, ever, he signed over rights to access to his kids and was heard of no more.'

'Which left Claire alone.'

'Yeah.' He stared into the middle distance, remembering her terror. Remembering his own fear. 'She had irreversible pulmonary hypertension, a contraindication for a heart transplant, but a transplant did end up buying her enough time to think about the boys' future without her. While she was ill her parents took her and the boys back into their home. She had enough time to accept the boys could never be happy with her parents as sole carers.'

'Why not?' Weirdly, once again she seemed detached. The way she was, he wouldn't be surprised if she produced a clipboard from her beach bag and started taking notes.

But her detached manner helped. He found himself wanting to outline the events that had propelled him here.

'Her parents are…overpowering,' he told her. 'Because we'd been friends for so long I already knew that. Claire had been pushed as a child, really pushed. Ballet, piano, violin, gym—polo, for heaven's sake—and she was expected to be brilliant at everything. To be honest, I suspect that's why she fell for Creepy Steve and the other creeps before him—it was a dumb attempt to rebel. I gather, after she fell ill, the relationship with her parents grew more strained. Anyway, even before she had the transplant she knew the odds—she knew she wasn't going to be around long-term for the boys. In the end she was desperate for me to have some influence in the way they were raised—so she asked me to marry her and adopt them.'

What followed was silence. Normally friends or colleagues jumped in at that point in the story. Not Rachel. She seemed to be taking her time to think it through.

'That was some ask,' she said at last. 'I can't imagine how it made you feel.'

'We were good friends,' he said diffidently. 'And it wasn't as if marrying and settling down was my style.' He gave a rueful smile. 'I worked, I surfed, I had fun. Family wasn't on my radar. And we thought—Claire and I both thought— that it'd be simple enough. If by some miracle she survived long-term then we'd divorce. If she died, then her parents would do the hard yards of parenting—they saw the boys as their responsibility and had already made it clear that's what they wanted. I'd just be around on the edges, giving them another long-term person for security, but with enough legal authority to step in if her parents pushed too hard.'

'Still, it's a big deal.'

'You wouldn't have done it?'

'You said marrying wasn't your style. It's so far off my radar it's another world. That kind of involvement—any kind of personal involvement—isn't my scene.'

'Really?' He eyed her curiously and once again that sense of a clipboard between them came into his mind. 'Yet last weekend you were there for me.'

'There wasn't a choice. Not that I minded. It was a finite commitment with the end in view. What you're describing… Long-term involvement seems a given.'

'There was no way I thought it'd interfere with my Friday nights though,' he said with another rueful look down at his beer. 'But look at me now.'

'So what happened?'

'She died,' he said simply. 'She tried for another transplant, which went horribly wrong— she was never going to be strong enough to deal with it and she knew it, but her parents were fighting with every means they had. When it was over the boys stayed living with them and I tried to take up where we'd left off, seeing them occasionally, taking them to soccer. Only it didn't work. The kids got quiet. You know the rule in Emergency? Triage? A kid comes in screaming its lungs out and a kid comes in limp and silent. Which one needs attention? The limp one every time, and they were limp.'

'So…a problem.'

'Claire had given me custody in her will,' he said. 'She didn't think I'd need it. All she'd asked is that I accept the power to override her parents if they did anything I knew she'd hate. So I kept hanging out with them, being a mate rather than a dad. But the months wore on and they kept getting quieter. I knew things weren't right, but I couldn't nail it.

'And then one night I went around and they'd just brought their school reports home. School reports for kids. Henry was in infant class. You know the kind of report? *Henry: A+ for finger painting, A+ for tying shoelaces.* But Kit, who was two years older, had a slightly more precise report. *Kit is struggling a little. B-for reading.* The housekeeper let me in, and I could hear a row. I walked into the study and Claire's dad had them lined up, waving reports in his hand and blasting Kit. Almost spitting into his face. *"You let a five-year-old beat you. What are you? A pansy? You take after your no-good father. No grandchild of mine lets a five-year-old beat him, you good-for-nothing little...'"*

He fell silent, remembering the sick horror as he'd realised what had to be done. By him.

Friday nights were the least of it.

'They'd been authoritarian with Claire in her childhood,' he said, speaking almost to himself rather than Rachel. 'That's why she worried, but she knew they loved her, and she thought they loved her boys. But when she died... I think their grief has left them a little unhinged. It doesn't help that the boys all have Steve's red hair—they look like him. I'm no psychologist but it seems there's a part of them that can't bear the boys to be...not Claire? I looked at them that night and saw no softness, only determination that the boys fall into line. And the things the old man said when I tried to defend them... It was almost like he was blaming the boys for her death.'

'So you stepped in.'

'It couldn't continue,' he said heavily. 'They were determined to keep control, but I had the authority and I had them out of the house almost before they realised what I was doing. That night we sat up and watched dumb movies and ate junk food and didn't talk about report cards once. I had a one-bedroom hospital apartment. They slept on the floor and I didn't hear a complaint. I was then hit by a battalion of lawyers, plus Charles and Marjorie practically hounding the boys. Losing control was unthinkable. They were at the school gates, demanding the boys come home with them. They were calling me everything under the sun...'

He broke off. It was too much to recall—his struggle to explain that if they'd just back off, give the boys a bit of space, let them be kids, then things could work. His realisation that it wasn't going to happen. The acceptance that his life had to change.

'In the end I knew it'd never work,' he said. 'I started looking for another apartment, but when the old man hired a couple of thugs to collect the kids from school, thugs who were prepared to see me off with force, I just...' He stopped, closed his eyes, then forced himself to go on. 'I quit at the hospital. I knew this place was here. My grandparents built this house and it still belonged to me. I knew Shallow Bay could use any doctor they could get, so here we are.'

'Safe,' she said softly, almost a whisper.

'Not quite safe,' he told her. 'Charles and Marjorie have applied for custody. Claire's death might have left them a little unhinged, but as blood relatives they have a case and they're powerful. They say their daughter was mentally unfit when she signed the adoption papers. I'm single, I work long hours, I need to use childminders. Regardless, my lawyers tell me they have little chance unless they can prove I'm an unfit parent. Which is why it's important they don't find out about Kit's hand.'

'That was hardly your fault.'

'They won't see it like that.' He was confronting his worries now. There was something about this place, this woman…

No. It was simply that there'd been no one to talk to for so long. With Rachel… She seemed dispassionate, almost like a psychoanalyst, letting him go where he willed with no judgement. It was a weird sensation and he wasn't sure why he was reacting to it, but the need to talk was almost overpowering.

'Marcus is too serious,' he told her. 'He blames himself for Kit's hand. He blames himself for everything. When his grandfather looked like he was about to hit Kit, Marcus shoved himself in between. 'Hit me instead,' he was yelling. 'My report's worse.' Only of course it wasn't, and afterwards he even asked me if he should try and fail a few tests at school to make Kit feel better.

'Henry's littler, less complicated, but he has nightmares. I carry a radio in my pocket. If I'm called out at night Rose listens in and so do I. It's not great, not even totally safe, but it's the best I can do when I've been on call twenty-four-seven. So Rose and I hear the minute he wakes and it's a race to see who can get there first. Because of what I do, it's usually Rose but he holds himself rigid, sweating, until I get there.'

He paused. Was he waiting for her to comment? She didn't, just watched him, waiting for him to continue.

He wasn't even sure if she was interested but... What was it with this woman?

'And then Kit,' he said. 'Left alone... Well, his cut hand is the least of it. Sometimes he wants me to be there for him, but not often. Tonight he hugged me, but that's unusual. There's a part of him that actively tries to drive me away. It's like he's testing me, expecting me to leave like his parents, thinking the sooner it happens the sooner he'll get it over with. So how do I break through that?'

Once again she didn't answer. He finished his beer and stared at the empty bottle. Rachel gazed out over the ocean, watching the water turn a soft tangerine with the reflections of the setting sun. Somehow she seemed to be melting into herself, folding, tucking herself neatly away—to where no one could touch her? To where personal stories didn't hurt?

'Your parents?' she said, almost absently, and why should he answer that? But he did.

'Loving but absent,' he told her. 'Overseas. Caught up in their careers. These kids have nothing to do with them.' And for the life of him he couldn't keep his voice from sounding bleak.

He heard it and he flinched. He sounded needy. Him. He didn't need anyone.

Except he did need help for the boys, and he didn't know where to begin to ask.

The silence stretched. It seemed they were both staring into the future. Or the past?

What was her story? She wasn't saying.

'Kids are resilient,' she said at last, breaking the spell. She stood up and brushed the sand from her legs. 'You're doing the best you can. They'll survive.'

'Like you survived?'

She froze at that. 'I don't know what you mean.'

'Cigarette burns,' he said neutrally. 'Unmistakable once you've treated them.'

'And none of your business.'

'So I spill my all to you…'

'And I don't spill back.' She shrugged. 'You've been generous but one low-alcohol beer does not a contract make. I need to go home. I'm hungry.'

'We have hamburgers at my place.'

A glimmer of humour returned and her lips twitched. 'So you're asking…what? You'll give me a hamburger in return for me being third man in Dragon Doom or whatever?'

'Hey, I never said…'

'You didn't need to. I guessed. So, no, thank you.' The smile was still there. 'I have home-made lasagne, which will heat while I'm in the shower. Then I have a date with a movie. So while Dragons are tempting, sorry. Bye.'

Home-made lasagne. A movie. Maybe a bottle of wine. It was like a siren's song and it was so far out of his list of possibilities that he couldn't even think about it.

He rose as well, aware of emptiness. Of leaving without her.

And then his phone vibrated.

He closed his eyes for a second, but this was almost inevitable, a call on Friday night. Why not?

He snagged his phone from his pocket. Unknown number. Local.

Work.

'Dr Lavery.'

'Doc? It's Col Hunter here.'

His phone was set on loudspeaker—he set it every night as he left work because of the times he had to listen over the racket the kids were making. Col's voice was deep and booming, disturbing the silence of the beach, but Tom left it on loud. After all, Rachel was a colleague.

'How can I help you?' Already he knew there was trouble. Underlying Col's booming voice he could hear pain.

'I fell over the pig,' Col managed. 'Got her in, got her fed, thought she had her snout in the trough and then suddenly she's shoving her way between me and the gate, trying to get out again. It's me 'taters she wants, Doc. Spent all bloody summer trying to get a decent crop. She's been watching me water 'em, fertilise 'em and now she wants 'em. Dutch Creams—the best 'taters you can get—and Mavis isn't bloody having 'em.'

'You've hurt yourself.' Cut to the chase, Col.

'It's me hip,' Col said. 'Had to crawl inside. Managed to get the sty gate shut though, so I won. Bloody pig.'

Tom almost grinned but didn't. Col was in his eighties and had suffered osteoarthritis for years. A fall, a damaged hip...

'Is there anyone with you?' he asked.

'You know Pat left me years ago,' Col managed. '"The pigs or me", she said and off she went with some life insurance fella. Kids are both in Melbourne. Doc, I can't seem to pull meself up. Reckon I need you, mate.'

'I reckon you do, too,' Tom told him. 'Your place is right up the top of Bellbird Ridge, right?'

'You got it. I remember you coming here with your grandpa when you were a little fella.'

'I'm coming again now,' Tom told him. 'It's probably best if you don't move until I get there.'

'You don't need to tell me that, Doc,' Col said. 'Passed out twice getting to the phone. Not risking that again. But...could you make it fast?'

'I'll make it fast,' Tom said. 'Grit your teeth, mate. I'm on my way.'

'I'll come with you.'

Where had that come from? She wasn't on call. She and Tom had sat down last Monday and defined their call duties. Tonight she was off—unless for emergencies.

This was hardly an emergency—an old man falling, possibly breaking a hip. Shallow Bay had an ambulance service of sorts, a vehicle equipped with stretchers, manned by volunteers trained in first aid. Tom could easily assess the damage and call her in if he needed her.

So why was she offering?

She had no idea. Maybe it was the slump of Tom's shoulders as he disconnected, a slump that spoke of regret.

Why, though? If he was back in Sydney she'd understand it. He'd be leaving his friends, his good time. Here, this call would mean little more than being home late for children who weren't his, children who were already being adequately cared for.

Except he did care. That was the part she was struggling with. Taking children from their grandparents when they were being obviously mistreated—that was understandable. He'd had no choice. But she'd met Rose. She knew that lady was a carer in a million. The boys were safe.

Tom had already confessed he didn't want to play their video game. This was the perfect excuse. So why the shoulder slump?

She didn't understand—but neither did she understand the imperative urge to help.

'Rachel, thanks, but I need to go now.' Tom was gathering the empty bottles, turning towards the track.

But she'd already hauled her dress over her swimsuit. She grabbed her beach bag and headed after him.

'I can cope,' he said as she fell in beside him. 'There's no need for you to come as well.'

'You have trained paramedics?'

'You know we don't, but...'

'But you're sure I'd be useless? Tom, I can get you home to the boys faster. I'd go by myself but I don't know the way and risk getting lost. Plus you've already told him you're coming and it sounds as if he knows you.'

'Everyone in Shallow Bay knows me,' he said.

He hadn't eased his stride to accommodate her but she was keeping up.

'Because you came here as a child?'

'The people here loved my grandparents,' he said, talking briskly as he walked. 'My grandpa cared for everyone. My grandmother wasn't a doctor but she cared even more. They only had the one child, my dad, but that didn't stop their house being stuffed to the plimsoll line with people in need, stray dogs, pot plants Grandma was looking after for people in hospital—whatever. I was supposed to have my own bedroom in the school holidays, but in the end I carved out a niche in the attic and called it mine. I told Grandma if ever I found a needy *anything* in there, animal, mineral or vegetable, I was heading straight back to Sydney.'

'Did you mean it?'

'Of course I didn't.'

'And now you're right back in the chaos.'

'As you say,' he said briefly.

They'd reached his car, parked outside his cottage. He paused. 'I'll duck in and tell Rose what's happening. But there *is* no need for you to come.'

'You don't want help?'

He gave her an odd look, as if considering.

Then he nodded. 'Of course. Two doctors are always better than one.'

'Which is why I'm here,' Rachel said. 'Instead of where we'd both be happier, back in Sydney.'

'Okay, then,' he told her and tossed her his phone. 'Accepted. Can you find "ambulance" in Favourites? Maggie coordinates the ambulance volunteers. Tell her we need a car up at Col Hunter's place. Probable fracture. No lights and sirens, though, take it easy.'

'Why not lights and sirens?' Surely there was a need for haste.

'Because our volunteers love lights and sirens,' he said grimly. 'And it's getting dark and the roads are narrow. Once upon a time I lived and breathed adrenaline but not any more. Shallow Bay might have two doctors now, Dr Tilding, but let's not go asking for trouble.'

# CHAPTER FIVE

ONE ELDERLY FARMER. One injured hip.

As soon as she saw him, Rachel knew she'd made the right call to accompany Tom. The old man's breathing was shallow and rapid, shock and pain taking their toll. She did the busy work, setting up an IV, organising oxygen, finding cushions and blankets to keep the old man as warm as possible until the ambulance arrived. Tom did the assessment—and the reassurance.

Tom was senior to her. She'd have been happy to take a back seat anyway, but Tom was offering more than medicine.

The old man reacted to his presence with humbling gratitude. 'Thank God you're here, Doc. I'll be right now.' She saw the absolute trust and she thought, that can't have developed solely in the time Tom's been a doctor here.

And then she thought of his grandfather, here for forty or more years. She'd read of his work when she'd accepted the scholarship. He'd been an old-fashioned family doctor, he and Tom's grandmother devoted enough to their community to set up the foundation that had sent her here.

And it seemed Tom had inherited that trust. He was Doc Lavery. Shallow Bay's own.

His grandparents would be proud of him, she thought. She watched his gentleness, his skill, and she thought Shallow Bay was blessed to have him.

But he didn't want to have Shallow Bay. He'd been forced to be here.

As she had—but Tom was here for life. Because of emotional ties.

She didn't have them. She didn't believe in them. They let you down, over and over.

Claire had trusted them absolutely when she'd placed her boys in Tom's care, she thought. The ties had obviously been bone-deep and he'd had no choice but to accept responsibility.

All this she thought as she worked in the background, preparing what Tom needed to make the old man comfortable. The ambulance arrived, two youngish volunteers, farmers by the look of them. Women who knew Col well. Who accepted orders willingly, yet who didn't have the training to do more than lift and carry and keep safe.

How alone had Tom been before she'd arrived?

How alone would he be when she left?

There'd be another scholarship holder to take her place, she thought. Another itinerant. Tom was here, where he didn't want to be. For ever.

They were supervising Col into the ambulance. The plan was for Tom to accompany Col to hospital while Rachel drove Tom's truck. Yeah, well, she was used to Moby Dick now. Her own little Petal was gleaming again, but Tom's SUV was far more sensible for the roads around here. He handed her the keys but took her arm, keeping her back for a moment, out of earshot of Col and his fussing attendants.

'Rachel, how do you feel about operating tonight?'

'Me?' She stared at him in surprise. 'Operate?'

'Sorry.' He gave a rueful shrug. 'Wrong wording. The operator would be me. You know I trained as an orthopaedic surgeon before my life went pear-shaped? When I came here I brought all the equipment I need. I've hardly used it. We're not set up for major surgery, but in this case… How do you feel about giving the anaesthetic while I operate?'

'Tonight?'

'It depends on the X-rays, of course,' he told her. 'But every indication is that he's fractured his hip. He's eighty-seven and he's frail, but he's mentally fine. He loves his farm. He'll want to get back here as soon as possible. You know the odds on morbidity after hip fracture. It depends so much on getting him back on his feet fast. If he's not upright in days, he may well never get back up. I'd like him to wake up tomorrow to Day One of recovery instead of Day One in Sydney, waiting for specialist assessment that may not happen until Monday. Cath from Ferndale will come if I need her, but she's a couple of hours' drive away. So…are you up for surgery?'

An anaesthetic for a shocked, elderly and frail man? She'd signed up for family medicine. This wasn't in her contract. She had boundaries.

But it seemed her boundaries had been crossed almost the moment she'd arrived in Shallow Bay. Tom was looking at her expectantly. The ambulance ladies were watching them both, wondering what the problem was.

One old man was lying in the ambulance and Tom was asking for her help.

So get a grip, she told herself. This was peanuts compared to what Tom had committed to this place. Besides, she'd done an anaesthetic rotation in her internship. She could manage.

'I read your CV,' Tom said. 'I know you have the skills.'

'You don't know how confident I am.'

'And you don't know how skilled I am. So... are we prepared to trust each other?'

And how was a woman to respond to that?

No! The question should be, How would a *doctor* respond? she reminded herself. This situation had nothing to do with her being a woman. It also had nothing to do with the way Tom was looking at her, those dark eyes watchful. Waiting to see if she'd help.

But when she nodded and said, 'Let's do it,' Tom nodded his relief. Those gorgeous eyes smiled at her and she was forced to smile back...

No! This was crazy. She was in the middle of a medical crisis. She had no business to be even conscious that a colleague was smiling at her.

But she was only human.

No, she thought as she beat back totally irrelevant thoughts. She was only a woman. And that woman needed to get herself back under control, fast.

He'd said he was surgically trained. He was so much more. What Rachel saw in the next couple of hours was a masterclass in surgical repair.

Col Hunter was a big man with big bones but those bones had been eroded by osteoarthritis. It wouldn't have taken a huge knock to break his femur. It did take a huge amount of skill to repair it, but Tom was up to it.

Rachel focused on the anaesthetic, which took concentration, especially as she was working from a basic skill set. Col was frail and the shock of the fall, plus what seemed to be the tail end of a bronchial infection, had her hauling up everything she'd ever learned and more.

But they had a full theatre complement. Roscoe had come in, as had a couple of other senior nurses. They'd obviously operated with Tom before, anticipating his needs, leaving the way clear for Rachel to concentrate solely on the job at hand.

She had a little space at the edges to watch what Tom was doing.

This man could make a fortune as an ortho-paedic surgeon, she thought. What a waste that he was stuck here, leaving those skills unused.

Except he was using them tonight. He worked swiftly, and Rachel thought Col couldn't have had better treatment if he'd been brought into a major city hospital.

As it was, he'd wake in a hospital he knew, sur-rounded by people he knew. With Tom's skill, he'd have a functional hip, far stronger than it'd been before the fall.

There was talk in the theatre, the banter that always went on between medical staff who knew each other well, but Rachel didn't contribute. Her silence was respected, though. Maybe the nurses as well as Tom knew how much she needed to focus on what she was doing.

Maybe they didn't notice that she was focus-ing just a little bit on Tom himself.

On his fierce concentration. On his skills. On the way he responded to the nurses around him.

Roscoe was anxious. He shouldn't be here— his wife's baby was overdue—but there was no way he'd have delegated tonight's surgery to someone junior. Tom chatted to Roscoe as he worked, including him, making him maybe even busier than he needed to be. It didn't deflect Tom's focus on the work at hand, but Rachel realised it was lessening the look of strain she'd been seeing on Roscoe's face for the last few days.

At last it was over. Col was being wheeled off to the ward next to the nurses' station. He'd be watched like a hawk all night, surrounded…by his own?

That was what it felt like, Rachel thought. These people…this community… It was almost family.

Left to herself, she headed into the scrub room, stripped off her gown and tossed it into the bin. And as she did she was aware of a sense of desolation.

A feeling she'd had often. A feeling of being on the outside looking in.

'Well done.' Tom had stayed behind in Theatre to write up orders. He entered the scrub room now and started stripping off himself. 'You're a real pro, Dr Tilding.'

'Not bad yourself, Dr Lavery. You really are an orthopod.'

'That's a past life,' he told her curtly and the way he propelled his gown into the bin had a bit more force than necessary. 'I'll operate in emergencies but not from choice. I'm now a family doctor.'

'I'm sorry.'

Rid of their theatre gear, they walked outside together. Rose had offered to stay and sleep with the boys for the night, but Tom would want to get home, Rachel thought. *She* wanted to get home. The image of community—family—was weirdly unsettling. She needed to be in her own cottage, with the door firmly shut, with the world safely at bay.

What was unsettling her wasn't just about medicine, she thought. In fact it was hardly about medicine at all. It was Tom greeting her on the beach, sitting beside her, telling her how his life had changed. Exposing his past. It was Tom seeing her scars and knowing immediately what had caused them. There'd be questions in his mind that she wasn't prepared to answer, but he hadn't pushed and somehow that consideration had pushed her even further out of her comfort zone.

For it was Tom himself who disturbed her. Tom, who'd given up his life in Sydney, his career as a surgeon, everything he most valued, to bring three kids somewhere they could be safe.

It was Tom of the crinkly dark eyes, with the smile that reached...something that hadn't been touched for a very long time.

Had it ever been touched?

They were out on the veranda now. It was a five-minute walk down to the cottages but Moby Dick was in the car park. 'Well done us,' Tom said softly into the stillness of the night. 'Thank you, Rachel. You did great. You want a ride home?'

'You did great yourself, and I can walk.'

'Then beware drop bears.'

Drop bears. The imaginary animal used by Aussies to tease tourists, by mums and dads to make kids go 'ooh' and cling tight as they walked under tall trees. She managed a smile. Drop bears weren't real.

But this night didn't feel real. For some reason Tom had her so... What was the word for it? She didn't have a clue. And she had no idea why she was feeling...what she was feeling.

'I hear the antigowobblers are bad at this time of year too,' she managed.

'The jabberwockies are pretty scary as well,'

he responded promptly. 'I haven't seen one for a while, but you can't be too careful.'

'Yeah, but I'll walk anyway.'

'Rachel, I won't hurt you.'

Why had he said that? She stilled while the ramifications of his words hit home.

'Why…why would I think you'd hurt me?'

'Because people have hurt you in the past. And it's still with you.'

'That was a long time ago,' she managed.

'But scars like that…'

'I don't want to talk about it.'

'There's no need to talk about it. Just know that I won't hurt you.'

'Th…thank you.'

'You were awesome tonight,' he said softly now, as if he knew that he'd scared her. 'You being here… The fact that we operated so fast… It may well make the difference as to whether Col walks again.'

'He should.'

'Thanks to both of us. We're a team.'

A team. She and Tom.

The concept was purely medical, she thought, but the way she felt… It was so much more.

But she said nothing.

Silence.

She should walk away, but her feet didn't seem to want to.

Nothing about her wanted to.

This was the back entrance to the hospital, dimly lit. The main entrance was on the town side. This veranda overlooked the ocean. Below them, they could see the shape of their cottages in the moonlight, with the lights on in Tom's living room. They could see the ribbons of moonlight beyond, rippling over the surface of the sea.

The silence seemed to be growing. There was nothing but the sound of the surf on the beach below.

There was nothing but each other.

A man and a woman.

And, looking at his face, she suddenly saw a side of Tom she'd never seen before. He was gazing down at the lights of his cottage and for a fleeting moment she saw something akin to panic. It was gone in an instant but she knew she'd seen it—and she knew what it was.

Behind him, in the hospital, was a small boy who was his responsibility, and waiting for him at home were two more.

As well as that, the hospital was full of the

same responsibilities. Rachel was under no illusions as to why Tom's grandfather had set up her scholarship. It was to force doctors to come here. This place was so remote, so far from any services, so far from the friends, the life Tom knew...

And yet he'd taken it on and would continue to look after them all. Until the boys were grown, his promise to his friend was unbreakable.

The look was gone now, hidden under the veneer of strength and commitment. He'd head back to his cottage, say goodnight to Rose, check on the children, go to bed.

But the memory of that look stayed with her, somehow searing itself into her mind.

He was trapped.

And, almost unbidden, before she even knew what she intended, she reached out and touched Tom's face. A feather touch. A touch of comfort? A touch to say she understood that look?

How could she have understood it—and what on earth possessed her to make her reach out? She'd never done such a thing. But she didn't pull back. Amazingly, the touch felt right.

She was a woman with boundaries, a woman who knew to keep herself to herself, and this was a man who seemingly had no boundaries. A man who collected strays and changed his life because of them. Who accepted that he was trapped for ever—because of a simple promise to a friend.

Was it wonder that made her reach out—as if touching a being from another world?

But it wasn't strangeness she was feeling. It was Tom's face. A face of strength. Of endurance.

Her fingers traced his cheekbones, feeling the stubble from a long day without a razor. Feeling his warmth. His familiarity? For it was as if she knew him. It was as if something inside her was responding to something she didn't understand. Something that maybe should have frightened her, and yet somehow didn't.

His hand raised and caught her fingers. And held. The fear should have been there—but wasn't.

'You did amazingly tonight,' Tom told her, and his voice was somehow an extension of the silence of the night. 'We both did well. Well done us.'

Medicine, she thought, and she knew why

he'd brought it back to that. They both needed to focus on work. It was what they did.

And then his hand tugged a little, pulling her body closer.

And with that came panic.

What was she doing here? Why had she touched? She never touched. She was suddenly hauling her hand back as if it burned, and he let her go instantly.

'Don't,' she said and she was stammering. 'Please. I should never... I'd never...' She was fighting to make her voice sound practical, acerbic, moving on. She'd watched love affairs spring up almost unbidden in the hothouse of medical workplaces, and when had any good come of them? And for her? It'd be a disaster.

'What are you frightened of?' His voice was gentle. He was watching her, quietly questioning. There was no pressure. She could turn and leave.

She should turn and leave, but it was she who'd instigated the contact. He deserved some explanation.

'I don't think... It's not me who's frightened,' she told him, struggling to make sense of what had happened. 'I just thought... For a moment it looked like you were afraid.'

'What would I be afraid of?'

'Of loving,' she said simply. 'Of being stuck with the boys because you think you love them.'

'I do love them.'

'But you're afraid of being trapped.'

'Well, the time for that's long over,' he told her, but he was watching her face and she had the sensation that he wasn't focused on the boys. He was focused solely on her. 'I'm committed and there's nothing I can do about it.'

'Then you shouldn't have let yourself care in the first place,' she blurted out. Almost instantly she regretted it. Who was she to say such a thing? It was none of her business. No one was her business.

'How can you stop caring?' He was watching her with eyes that seemed to see far more than she wanted them to see. 'How did you stop caring, Rachel Tilding?'

'I didn't. It's just… I don't get involved.'

'And yet you looked after my boys in an emergency. You couldn't walk away.'

'I accept responsibility when I must. That's not caring.'

'It seems like it to me.'

'It's not.' She sounded panicked, she knew she did, but there was nothing she could do about it.

'Is caring something to be frightened of?'

'Yes!' And how exposed did that make her feel?

'It shouldn't be.' His hand came out and took hers again, and his fingers slid up her wrist. She'd unbuttoned her cuffs and rolled up her sleeves before donning scrubs. She'd rolled them down again but her cuffs had stayed unfastened.

Now his hand slid up her arm, still gently. She could pull away but it was as if she was paralysed. She just…let him.

The scars were all above her elbows. Never below. Her stepfather had learned that early—if he hurt her where it could be seen then trouble followed.

Tom's fingers found them. Traced them.

His eyes asked questions she knew he wouldn't voice.

She could step away. She could keep her boundaries in place. But something seemed to be breaking and she didn't have a clue what to do about it.

'Who?' he asked gently and the question hung.

Walk away or tell him? Suddenly there was no choice.

'My stepfather,' she said at last, because the need to tell him was suddenly almost overwhelming. 'Stepfathers aren't always like you. Burning me was less effort than hitting me.'

'Rachel…' It was an appalled whisper, a whisper that made her flinch.

'They're old scars,' she told him, speaking too fast, wanting to get it over with. 'And it stopped. When I was eleven the school sports uniform changed, to capped sleeves instead of longer ones. I stuck to the old uniform until my gym teacher felt sorry for me and gave me one out of lost property. She insisted I put it straight on. I can still remember her face. I remember being terrified because of all the things my stepfather told me would happen if anyone found out, but in the end it was my escape. The school called the police and I didn't have to see him any more. Then there were foster homes. Decent food and clothes. Space to study. All the things I craved.'

'Your mother?'

That was the hard bit, but somehow she made herself continue. 'She…she stayed loyal to him,' she told him and even now it felt appalling to say.

'Even when he went to prison. But it was fine. I was looked after. I'd escaped. Not like you.'

'You can't compare my situation to yours,' he told her, still horrified. 'Not in a million years.'

'I wouldn't,' she said. 'But I'd never be in your situation. I never let myself care. I do what I have to do.'

'Out of duty? Why don't I believe that?'

'It's true. I accept responsibility but I never take it further.'

'So when you touched me then?'

'I felt sorry for you.'

'Really? Was that all it was?'

'Yes!' Emotion was threatening to overwhelm her. She wrenched her arm back, snatching it against her chest as if it hurt.

'I won't hurt you,' he said.

'You keep saying that. I don't for a minute think you're capable of hurting me.'

'Do you equate the two?' he said almost casually. 'Caring and hurting?'

'You're not my shrink.'

'I wouldn't want to be your shrink. I'm a surgeon. I see what's inside people's bodies, not their heads. But hell, Rachel, what you've lived through…'

'Leave it,' she said roughly.

'And leave you? You've just spilled your secret to me. Will you go home and sleep tonight?'

'I've slept after far worse,' she snapped and then bit her lip. What was she doing, exposing herself like this?

'It's not bad, telling people what happened,' he said, his eyes still watchful. Still caring? 'What happened to you was bad. Talking to someone who could be a friend should surely be the opposite.'

'I don't…do friends.'

'Then maybe you should.'

His hands caught hers again. Two strong hands holding hers. Warmth holding cold. Steady holding shaking.

Man holding woman.

'You're a strong, vibrant woman,' he said firmly now, as if he needed to convince her. 'You've come through a war and out the other side, and you need to get on with life. But life involves sharing. Caring. It involves warmth, passion, all the things you're most scared of.'

'I'm not scared.'

'Really?'

And then there was silence. A long silence. It

stretched into the night, not peaceful but some-how not threatening either. It was a moment where the world seemed as if it could shift either way—it couldn't decide.

And then Tom said, 'I'd like to kiss you.'

Well, there was the signal to run. There was the signal to get off the veranda fast, to retreat to her cottage and bolt the door behind her.

But his hands still held. Gently, though. She could pull away if she wanted.

But his eyes held her too, and that was a link she couldn't break. She was gazing up at him in the moonlight, at this charismatic man, at warmth, compassion, strength, empathy.

Caring.

Everything she'd been afraid of for ever was right here and she couldn't break away.

She simply stood while his statement hung.

*I'd like to kiss you.*

She had to say no, but the word wouldn't come. His eyes held and held and held. The stillness of the night. The peace. The feel of this man's hands.

'Yes, please,' she heard herself whisper and then he kissed her, and the night melted into oblivion.

* * *

What was he doing?

This was a colleague, a woman he'd met only one week before. More, she was damaged, scarred, not only physically but mentally. That meant she was needy and heaven keep him from more need. He should be quietly sympathetic, empathetic even. He should talk to her about counselling alternatives—and then he should step away.

Instead he was drawing her close. Her breasts were moulding against his chest. He was tilting her chin—and he was kissing her.

And the moment his mouth met hers…

Something.

Some indefinable something. Some connection he hadn't felt in all the years he'd dated.

Maybe it was the night, the stillness, the calm, the beauty of the scene around them. Maybe it was the way he felt about her, the sense that she'd been so badly hurt. Maybe it was that he felt appalled, horrified for her.

But maybe it was none of those things. Maybe it was the way her mouth seemed to melt against his. Maybe it was the curve of her body. Maybe it was the tiny murmur she gave as his mouth touched hers.

Maybe it was because he felt her surrender.

And it was surrender. He'd been watching her, talking to her, feeling his way, and he'd sensed fear. He'd seen boundaries she'd never crossed. But like a wild kitten enticed by food, by whispers, by warmth, he'd seen the temptation to trust. He'd seen her let slip boundary after boundary as she'd spoken to him.

And then she'd whispered acquiescence to this kiss and the last of the boundaries had fallen away and she was in his arms.

Not needy though. No longer needy. She was kissing him right back. Her hands went to the small of his back, holding him, claiming him as much as her mouth was claiming his.

And the kiss…

It was as if a spark had ignited a force he'd never expected, a force that held and held and held.

This woman. This night.

There were no barriers now. There was no room for backgrounds, for discussion of past wounds, of current responsibilities. Everything had fallen away in the face of this wonder.

For that was it—wonder. This kiss was almost one of primeval desire. They were two people who'd forgotten what they needed most but had suddenly found it. Two people who weren't letting go.

Neither could break away. Why should they? This was time out of frame, a wondrous moment snatched almost from life. The feel of her…the taste of her…

How could someone he'd known so briefly feel so right in his arms? How could her surrender feel so right?

It was as if his world was changing yet again, a seismic shift, a shift where his heart felt it could stretch again.

And with that thought…

'Doc? You still out there?'

It was a voice from behind the screen door. Roscoe.

'I have Col's daughter on the phone from Sydney,' Roscoe was calling. Heaven knew whether he'd seen what they were doing, but his voice sounded prosaic. Matter-of-fact. 'We left a message earlier when we couldn't raise her, but she's called back now. She wants to speak to you. If you aren't busy.'

And in those last four words Tom heard a trace of humour. So they'd been sprung. Great; it'd be all over the hospital—all over the town—by the morning.

'Roscoe...' He pulled reluctantly back from Rachel. His hands still held hers. He was still half in wonder.

'Shall I tell her you're busy?' Roscoe boomed, laughter surfacing.

'Go,' Rachel said, and finally she tugged her hands from his. 'I... I need to go myself. Good-night, Tom and...thank you.'

And before he could stop her she'd turned and headed down the steps, onto the track to the cottages. He let her go—there was no choice—but he stood and watched as she made her way into the dark.

'She'll be all right by herself,' Roscoe said as finally he turned to go back inside. 'She's a woman who's used to coping alone.'

How much had Roscoe seen?

'You need to get home yourself,' he said abruptly. 'If that baby of yours doesn't arrive in the next couple of days...'

'Yeah, change the subject, why don't you?'

Roscoe said, smiling. 'But you're right. Moving on. It's what we all have to do.'

What had she done?

Kissed Tom Lavery, that was what she'd done. Started an affair with a man who was technically her boss? Who was lumbered with three children he didn't want? Which was total anathema to her, after everything she'd taught herself.

She walked steadily down the track to her cottage, achingly aware of the man she'd left behind. It was all she could do not to run.

One kiss does not make an affair. She told herself that, and then, when she was sure she was out of earshot, she said it out loud. 'It was a kiss, nothing more. Heaven knows how many women he's kissed.'

But her...

She'd kissed—or been kissed—before this. Of course she had, but every time she'd pulled away. She didn't want the complications that went with any type of relationship.

But tonight she'd almost invited the kiss. He hadn't pushed himself on her. He'd asked and she'd agreed.

Because she'd wanted.

And that was what scared her most. She, Rachel Tilding, had suddenly wanted more than anything in the world to be kissed by Tom Lavery. And when that kiss had happened...

Her fingers crept to her lips. They felt full, swollen, the taste of the kiss still with her.

She wanted more?

'No!' she said out loud too, as the ramifications of what she'd done hit home. She was stuck in this place, as was Tom. She had no doubt that if he'd been back in Sydney he wouldn't have looked twice at the likes of her.

Had he kissed her because he felt sorry for her?

She reached her cottage, stepped inside, locked the door behind her and then leaned against it.

She was suddenly shaking.

'Get over it,' she told herself. Who needed a shrink when she had her own inner voice telling her what was sensible, telling her what she had to do to cope? 'It was just a kiss. Don't make a big deal of it. If you don't make a fuss, neither will he. Move on. Stay separate. To act like it was anything else would be...needy.'

And she wasn't needy. She was never needy.

But still she leaned on the door until the shakes subsided. Until she had herself back together.

Until she knew quite definitely that such a thing would—could—never be repeated. Her boundaries were up again, and they needed reinforcement.

So...

She made herself a mug of tea and headed to the internet, downloading a pdf of the latest research into post-polio syndrome. One of the elderly farmers she'd seen in clinic today showed every sign and she needed to research.

Work. Study. Medicine. It was her escape, her salvation—the only thing that mattered.

Tonight had changed nothing.

# CHAPTER SIX

TOM HADN'T EVEN made it to bed before the phone rang again. This time it was Roscoe, and his voice was about an octave higher than his normal gruffness.

'It's Lizzy.' Tom could hear his voice shaking. 'I've just come home and she's in full labour. She didn't want to worry us when she knew we were concerned about Col, but contractions are five minutes apart. Hell, Doc… We're coming in.'

He didn't bother to wake the sleeping Rose or the boys, just headed back to the hospital, praying things would go okay.

He hated delivering babies here. Without specialist backup, with so far to travel to the nearest paediatric services, he felt incredibly alone. Shallow Bay mums were advised to stay in Ferndale or go to Melbourne or Sydney a few weeks before their due date, but they hardly ever did. The impossibility of leaving families, of paying for accommodation… They preferred to put their faith in Tom.

Which made him feel sick with responsibility. Births meant two patients, not one, and if things went pear-shaped one doctor wasn't enough. At least he had Rachel now, and he headed back to the hospital praying he wouldn't need her.

Roscoe Junior, however, gave no cause for grief. He arrived just before dawn, informing the entire hospital of his displeasure at his eviction. Exhausted, aching for sleep, Tom walked back outside to face the morning.

Rachel was walking up the track towards him.

He saw her hesitate for a moment, pausing as if regrouping. And then she deliberately start walking again. A new day, a new attitude?

It didn't feel like a new day, and the memory of that kiss was still with him.

'Good morning,' she said formally, and he answered her in kind.

'Good morning to you too.' Their greetings somehow seemed like the set-up between fencers as they prepared to duel. *En garde.*

'Trouble?' she asked as she reached the veranda. She'd be taking in the fact that he looked like a train wreck. He needed a shower, clean clothes, sleep. But Rachel's tone was profession-ally interested, nothing more. The emotion of the night before was obviously in the past.

'Roscoe has a son,' he told her. 'Born an hour ago. Still protesting. All's well.'

'That's great. I'll check on them both at ward round.' She smiled but it wasn't the smile he re-membered.

She was back to distant.

'They're okay. No stitches. A straightforward birth, thank God. Lizzy's tired but happy. Ros-coe's dazed and proud fit to burst. Bub's great. There's not a lot for us to do.'

'Sleep for you,' she said. 'I'll take over.'

'If you would. I need to relieve Rose and let her go home. I've promised Kit he can come home today. I'll bring the boys up with me to collect him later.'

'And then spend the rest of the day super-vising?' Her brow creased. 'It's Saturday. No school. No childminder. No sleep?'

'I can cope without it.'

'We do what we have to do,' she said enigmati-cally. And then she took a step back and looked him over, making no pretence that she wasn't doing a full assessment. 'You look like something the cat dragged in.'

'Thanks,' he said dryly. 'Is that a medical diagnosis for free?'

'Yes and you're welcome. You need to do something about it.'

'So what should I take, Dr Tilding? Any free advice while you're at it?'

'Rest.'

'Like that's going to happen.'

She chewed her lip in the way he was starting to recognise. As if she was weighing up options. 'If you fall over you're no use to anyone.'

'I've had these boys for a year and I haven't fallen over yet.'

'That's like jumping from a high-rise and shouting "I'm okay so far" on the way down.'

He sighed. 'Rachel, there's not a thing I can do about it. At least you're here now. The weeks since your predecessor left have been hell, but knowing you can share the medical stuff is wonderful.'

'That's what I'm paid for,' she said bluntly, but she was still looking at him with doctor's eyes. Eyes that were seeking information. Eyes that fronted a medical mind, used to diagnosing and making decisions based on facts.

'Right,' she said. 'Here's your treatment regime.'

'You're giving me a treatment regime?'

'I am, and I'm not even charging you for it. And before you get any ideas that this is a personal favour—or even anything to do with last night, which it assuredly isn't...' She hesitated and bit her lip. 'Tom...you know last night was an aberration.'

'An aberration?'

'That's right. Not to be repeated. I'm treating it as a warning and so should you. This morning I've woken up perky and ready to move on.'

'Perky?' he said faintly. He looked at her, in her black trousers and long-sleeved shirt, her curls tugged tightly back with a simple band, her businesslike pumps—and he thought *perky* wasn't the word he'd use for her. And then he thought... *Perky's under there somewhere.*

Maybe that was the Rachel he'd kissed last night.

But that Rachel wasn't here now. This Rachel was all business.

'You know darned well that if you're exhausted

you make mistakes,' she told him. 'And as your colleague I'd be sharing them. So, because of that, and only because of that, I'm offering to take the boys this afternoon. Only if I'm not caught up here, though,' she added hastily. 'We both know there are no guarantees in this business. But it's Saturday so there's no clinic. I'll do a ward round and there are two house calls outstanding but after that I should be free. So the plan is that as soon as I'm available I'll take the boys to the beach while you sleep. Kit should be right for that, no?'

'He should,' he agreed faintly. 'The stitches are out. Salt water might even help.'

'There you go then. Sorted. You do the kids' morning shift and I'll be there as soon as I can.'

'Rachel...'

'Yes?'

He had to say it. 'The boys... They think you're a bit severe. They might not want to come with you.'

That set her back a bit. For a moment he saw a trace of grimness in the set of her mouth, but she moved on briskly. 'Are you giving them a choice? I can handle kids. Tell them to expect sausage rolls and chocolate cakes.'

'Sausage rolls and chocolate cakes...' he said faintly, thinking about timelines. 'How...?'

'I'll make mini microwave chocolate cakes while I have lunch,' she told him. 'I have pastry in the freezer. I can buy meat on the way home from house calls and sausage rolls are a snap. My splinter skill, Dr Lavery, is cooking. And, severe or not, I'm not into scaring small boys. Yes, I was forceful while I stayed with them, but the house was a muddle and they had Rose to do the warm and cuddly. I was there to work. So you can tell them that it's me and the beach or me glaring them into silence in your living room while you sleep. So, Dr Lavery...agreed?'

To say he was disconcerted would be an understatement. Here, when he'd least expected it, was another of her extraordinary offers.

She'd said she wasn't cuddly and she wasn't. She was prickly, defensive, damaged. And yet it wasn't exhaustion that had impelled her to touch him last night. It wasn't exhaustion that had made her want to melt into him.

She'd stepped in today for purely practical purposes. He accepted that. He was so weary he was at the point where any medical decisions he made would be suspect and, as his colleague, Rachel's offer could be seen as purely practical.

And yet… He looked at her, a neat, compact, efficient, self-contained—and cute—package, and he thought of all the effort that had gone into putting that package together. He'd read her scholarship application. She'd left school at fifteen with no support, working while studying online. How she'd made the grades for medical school was a miracle all on its own. And suddenly there were questions all over the place.

And, before he knew what he was about, he asked, 'Rachel, why did you decide to be a doctor? It must have been so hard. What made you want it so much?'

The question was totally divergent from what they'd been talking about. He'd taken them both aback. 'What's that got to do with anything?' she demanded, and he struggled to find an answer.

'Nothing,' he told her at last. 'I just… Well, I want to know.'

For a moment he thought she'd brush him off, push the question aside, head into the hospital to the relative sanctuary of work. He was starting to know this woman now. Medicine was her haven. Would she retreat to that now?

But, strangely, her chin was tilting upward and her eyes met his in challenge. There was a moment's silence while she thought about it and then she answered. With a challenge.

'You first.'

What the...? How had that happened? One moment they were saying good morning, the next moving to the intensely personal? And he'd started it.

So, how to answer?

That he'd been bright academically. That it had pleased the grandpa he'd loved. That he knew medicine would challenge him—and he also knew it made money? That he liked rescuing things, fixing things.

He could say all those things and they'd be true. But Rachel was watching, and he was suddenly aware that there was a deeper truth—and maybe she deserved it.

It was a truth that he'd hardly acknowledged to himself, but it was tucked away in the recesses of his memory and under Rachel's challenging gaze it suddenly resurfaced.

'When I was eight years old I was staying here with my grandparents for the school holidays,' he told her. 'Grandpa took me with him to do a house call, up on the ridge. The dad had had a tractor accident and was recuperating, so it was a simple house call for Grandpa and I was sent out to play with the kids. Then one of the littlies ran into the bush and met a brown snake. He stood on it and froze—and he was bitten. Not once. Several times. He collapsed almost straight away and by the time Grandpa got antivenom on board it was too late. He died within half an hour.'

'Oh, Tom…' Her eyes were still on his face. She didn't look horrified, though. She was a trained doctor. She'd have seen enough tragedies to stay calm in the face of such a story.

He was trying to match her calmness as he told her.

For some reason he'd never talked of it before. Why should he? After all this time he should hardly recall it himself. So why?

'It was the type of tragedy you and I have both seen and Grandpa was a doctor with years of experience,' he told her. 'And I scarcely knew what death was. Us kids were hustled out of the way by a neighbour who'd heard the screams and come over to help. I was aware that something big had happened, but I had no concept of its enormity. But I remember Grandpa's face as we drove home. Tight. Hard. He used to chat to me all the time but there was no chatting that day. And then, halfway home, he suddenly pulled over, cut the engine, put his head on the wheel and sobbed like a child. I remember him sitting there, his whole body shaking, and for me it was like the world was imploding. This was Grandpa. A rock. Grandpa, who could fix everything.'

'The best of us crack sometimes,' Rachel said neutrally, but softly, and he thought…hadn't her own adults let her down? And how much worse was the way they'd done it?

He wanted to make this about her—but he'd started the story and he had to finish.

'I don't know how long he cried,' he told her. 'It seemed an age but it was probably only minutes. Finally he pulled back and mopped up and turned to me. I have no idea how I remember it so well, but I can still hear him.

'"Tom, there are always tragedies in life. There are snakes and accidents and illnesses with no cure. We have to accept them. But Tom, if you can make a difference… If I'd had antivenom with me today instead of having to get someone to bring it up… If I'd had the skills… Tom,

I don't know what you'll do with your life but today you saw what happens when the resources aren't there. No matter what you do—baker, banker, artist, whatever you decide to be—just think about what difference you can make. If you're a banker give loans to people who need them. Make bread that'll make people feel like they've had a feast. Paint paintings that'll make people smile. Because you never know. Make a difference, Tom, and that's all I'm going to say.' And then we drove on and we never talked about it again.'

Silence. She was studying him, her face impassive. Still assessing? 'So medicine...'

'That day stayed with me,' he said simply. 'All the other reasons—knowledge, money, interest—they were the obvious reasons but there was always that day.'

Enough. What was he doing, talking like this, exposing himself? It must be weariness, he thought.

'Anyway, that's me. Now you.'

'Money?' she said quickly—too quickly. 'Security. All the things I never had as a child.'

'So why not law or commerce?'

Her chin tilted again, as if in defiance, and he

thought, She's not going to tell me. The armour's back in place.

But she didn't look away. They stood facing each other in the weak morning sunlight, and it was as if there was some sort of invisible line between them. Or two lines.

He'd crossed his already, he thought. Would she?

'Safety was one thing,' she said. 'Plus... accepting responsibility.'

'Sorry?'

'That's what medicine means to me. Safety.'

'You mean you'll never be without a job? Never without an income?'

She shook her head, closing her eyes for a moment, and he thought, She's going to pull back.

'Fair's fair,' he told her. 'If you really don't want to tell me...'

And he watched her hesitate and then decide to let it out.

'Medicine did mean safety,' she said in a voice that was little more than a whisper. 'But not economic. Mine's a childhood memory too. My mother...she wasn't the best. Social welfare was called often when I was little. They came once after... Well, it'd been a bad time for

Mum and I was obviously in a bit of a state. So they picked me up and took me to the hospital. I stayed there for a week. I remember doctors and nurses, staff who stayed when Mum came, who told her they'd be watching us, that if I came to them in that condition again, I'd be taken away and she could even go to jail. They were people who accepted responsibility for my welfare. And after that things got better.

'Then my stepfather arrived on the scene and it was awful again. The doctor who examined me when the teachers called the police... She did it again—she accepted responsibility for my safety. She moved heaven and earth to get my stepfather jailed. Me into foster care.

'It still wasn't over, though. There was always trouble. I told you Mum supported my stepfather when he went to jail? Well, she blamed me for that. She'd find me, yell invectives, make a scene. I was trouble for any foster parent who'd take me on. It messed with the other kids they had responsibility for, and I always had to move. In the end I fended for myself. But once... I cut my foot and it was infected. In the end I was scared enough to go to a medical clinic and the doctor there... She didn't just treat my foot. She gave me the number for crisis accommodation, the address of food vans. She let me use her phone. Then she said whenever I was in trouble to come to her, and she meant it. She accepted responsibility for me, and you can't begin to understand how that feels.' Her voice trailed off. 'And I thought then... To be like her... I couldn't, of course, but I'd get as close as I could.'

He was cringing inside. What she'd gone through... Yet there were still questions. 'Rachel, what she did...what all those people did... that's personal,' he said gently. 'You want to do radiology? Surely that's one of the most impersonal of medical careers.'

'So I'm not asking for miracles,' she said bluntly. 'I want to *be* a doctor. I want to accept responsibility for outcomes. But I can't *feel* like... well, like you seem to do. Accepting responsibility is one thing. Caring, though... Gut caring... That's something that's been wrung out of me long ago, if it ever existed in the first place.'

'So when you touched me last night...'

'An aberration,' she said briskly. 'A primeval urge, probably inherited from some dumb ancestor who owned a dog with all four legs and the ability to look cute. Anyway, that's that. Time to get on with the morning.'

Confidence ended. She gave a decisive nod and walked up the steps and past him. The steps were narrow and he felt the faint brush of her body as she passed.

He wanted to reach out.

No! This woman was complicated, needy, wounded. Surely the last thing he needed in his life was anything or anyone else who was complicated, needy or wounded.

And she didn't want or need to be rescued. She'd rescued herself.

Rose would be waiting to go home. Henry and Marcus would be waiting. He had to collect Kit. Hell, even Tuffy would be needing a walk. Why had he ever agreed to take on a rescue dog? He had enough problems.

So back off, he told himself. Rachel Tilding had scars that must be bone-deep, but she had them in hand. He needed to take a lesson from her attitude to life. Rachel had accepted some of his responsibility and he was grateful. That didn't mean he needed to feel anything else.

Feeling…anything else…might make life very complicated indeed.

\* \* \*

Her ward round was brisk, businesslike, professional, because that was how she needed to be. But she didn't feel like that inside. The time on the veranda had left her totally discombobulated.

How had they got so personal? Why had she told him so much about her past? It surely would have been enough to tell him she wanted the most secure profession she could find.

Except Tom had told her his story, and somehow she knew those feelings were usually protected as tightly as her own. Somehow his level of honesty had demanded the same of her.

And now she'd promised to take on three kids for the afternoon. When she'd planned to paint her bedroom.

She'd always planned her time off meticulously, knowing from past experience that idleness left room for depression. This weekend was for painting. Her little cottage was only her home for two years, but someone had once hung paintings in her bedroom, the marks were still there and it was annoying her.

Kids and beach instead?

It was okay. She needed to do ward rounds now and then house calls and shopping and preparation. Then she needed to collect the boys and supervise.

Which was okay because, for some reason, she didn't want time to think, to remember Tom's face as he'd told her his story. And also…she didn't want to think of his face as she'd told hers.

The man cared.

She didn't want his care. She didn't want anyone's care and she didn't want to care back. Hadn't she learned the hard way where care led? She accepted responsibility when she needed to, because that was what good people did, but that was as far as it went.

So. Work. Now. She could hear Roscoe Junior starting a lusty protest. Maybe there was a problem. Had Tom had time for a full examination?

A baby crying as lustily as this could scarcely have problems, but Roscoe and Lizzy might be worried. A full medical examination could reassure them, and she would hardly have time to think about Tom when she was focused on a newborn and his anxious parents.

And that was what she needed. No time to remember the look of compassion on Tom's face. No time to think about the way his hand had reached out to her as she'd finished her story.

And the way he'd looked down at his hand and then carefully pulled it back.

He'd made a decision, and she concurred.

There'd been enough emotion in both their pasts to last a lifetime. The last thing either of them needed was...to care.

# CHAPTER SEVEN

WORK WAS NEVER a problem for Rachel. Work was Rachel Tilding's safe place, her time for blocking out the problems of the world.

She moved swiftly through the ward rounds and then made two house calls just as efficiently. Yes, Edith Carey wanted to show Rachel her entire collection of woolly caps she'd knitted for next winter's charity drive but admiring three—and agreeing on a cash donation for more wool—was enough.

Entertaining small boys and thus ensuring Tom had some sleep was a medical priority. She had no use for a colleague who was asleep on his feet. So she swept through the morning's work with speed. She did a fast shop, an even faster cook and then went to collect the boys.

Tom greeted her when she arrived, but his greeting was wary. As was her response. She backed away fast, and he seemed relieved to see her go.

'Enjoy yourselves,' he told the boys and his smile encompassed her, but briefly. 'Thank you.'

'Think nothing of it,' she told him, turning away as the boys zoomed out of the door and made a fast track to the beach. They might be wary of her but the beach was like a siren song, not to be resisted, even if it meant a childminder they were unsure of.

'I appreciate this,' Tom told her, but she didn't respond. She'd moved on to childminding mode and Tom was no longer on her radar.

Or he shouldn't be. He needed sleep. That was the only reason she was doing this. Medical need. Once the boys—and Tuffy—were heading down the track with her towards the beach, she closed her mental door firmly behind him.

She was here to do a job.

And, as far as jobs went, what followed was satisfactory, her planning more than paying off.

She sat on the beach and supervised while the boys and Tuffy whooped in the shallows, explored the rock pools, acted as if they hadn't seen the beach for years. They devoured her cupcakes and sausage rolls in two swoops on the picnic basket. They had little need of her, which was just the way she liked it.

And then, when things started to lag a little, when they started playing nearer to her, when she sensed they were starting to feel a bit needy, she produced her pièce de résistance.

During the time she'd been here, Shallow Bay's General Store had had a beach display in the window, buckets and spades, things kids could mess around with on the beach. Included were plastic figures seemingly welded onto minia-ture surf boards, characters about a hand-span high. The figures were labelled with names like Surfer Sue or Hang-Ten Ted or Rip-Tide Roger. She'd seen a family using these on the beach a few days back and this morning, on impulse, she'd bought three.

As backup. Which she now produced.

Their function was to be thrown out into the shallows. Internal weights righted them as soon as an incoming wave hit. The little figures then rode gamely in, standing tall. The boys pounced on them with glee as they hit the beach, then threw them out again, searching for waves that'd provide a longer ride. Great. She could retreat to caretaker mode again.

Tom could have a little more sleep.

Except he couldn't, because suddenly he was

standing right behind her. She hadn't seen him approach. The boys were in the water and all her attention was on them.

'How's it going?' Tom asked and the unexpectedness of his voice made her jump. It was simply a startle reflex, she told herself. Her heart rate should settle again.

Except it didn't.

'F-fine,' she managed. 'You should be asleep.'

'I've had three hours. Luxury,' he told her. He was watching the boys, who hadn't noticed him. 'What are they doing?'

'Competing. Plastic surfers. Wipe-Out Wally. Tip-Off Tony. Grommet Georgie. They're trying to see whose goes furthest. Sadly, Henry's too little and Kit is one-handed. Marcus can throw further so he's winning by a country mile. They don't mind, though. They seem to be having fun.'

'You bought them plastic surfers?' he asked in a strange voice, still watching them.

'It gives me space to read.' She motioned to the medical journal beside her, which she'd been glancing at when the boys were out of the water. 'I know hardly anything about diseases animals can give you, and I'm thinking if I'm in the country for two years I should find out more. Did you know bats carry lyssavirus? They can give it to livestock, horses in particular, and it can be passed on. Symptoms...'

'I know the symptoms,' he told her. 'I read up on it when I got here. No case so far, touch wood.'

'When do you get time for reading?'

'When the boys are asleep. Or when my very kind neighbour takes them to the beach. Thank you for buying...what did you say?'

'Wipe-Out Wally. Tip-Off Tony. Grommet Georgie. They were the last on the shelf,' she admitted. 'Hang-Ten Ted and Surfer Sue must have been sold as soon as they arrived. These guys are the losers.'

'They're not losing now,' Tom said, watching the little figures wobbling in on the waves and the boys whooping encouragement as they neared the shore. 'You want to come down and see if we can beat Marcus?'

'They're busy,' she said shortly. 'They don't need us.'

'They might like us.'

'If you're taking over childminding, I'll read this.'

'Let's assume that one Shallow Bay doctor

has a good grip on lyssavirus and the other now knows the basics. Surely that's enough?' He stooped and snagged a cupcake from her picnic basket. 'Wow, these are excellent. Well done, Dr Tilding. But work's done. Surely now it's time to have fun yourself. Let's see if we can outdo Marcus.'

'Why, when they're happy?' she asked. 'You should be sleeping some more, or reading, or taking the time to catch up on what needs doing.'

'But what needs doing most?' he asked gently. 'Sleeping, reading, working—or forging a relationship with kids who need it?'

She looked up at him curiously. His eyes were challenging. Why?

'Surely these kids don't need more relationships,' she said, feeling puzzled. What was he on about? Making the kids dependent on him? 'Haven't they already learned that? A father who's deserted them? A mother who's dead? Why try and build more bonds that'll eventually break and cause heartache?'

'Because I want to?' He turned to watch the boys again, talking almost to himself. 'Yeah, weird, but the thing is... I've learned to love these guys. Without love, this whole set-up would be a disaster but, as it is, I get home and they greet me with what's starting to be just normal kid acceptance of a parent. Like I'm their foundation. Isn't that the most important thing I can give them?'

'There's no such thing as foundations,' she said shortly. 'Soon enough they'll have to launch themselves out into a world that doesn't give a toss. They need to be resilient, not reliant on pseudo-foundations that can crumble at any moment.'

'Hey!' Tom said, sounding startled. He turned back and looked down at her. 'That sounds like Life for Beginners, when right now you should be immersed in Beach for Beginners. You're overthinking. Bottom line is that I might enjoy whipping Marcus in the surfing game. So... I'm inviting you to watch. Take off those sandals, Dr Tilding, and come paddle.'

'I don't need...'

'This isn't about need. This is about fun. No strings attached.'

'I don't want...'

'How do you know what you want unless you try?'

'Tom...'

'Just come,' he said gently and then, even more gently, 'I dare you.'

His eyes met hers, a challenge, a hint of laughter. A hint of understanding.

Oh, those eyes. She should run. She should...

'Fine,' she snapped before she could stop herself. She tugged off her sandals, almost angrily. 'But just for a few minutes. Now you're here to take over, I'll go home.'

'Back to work.'

'I need to finish this journal.'

'Lyssavirus waits for no man,' he said solemnly. 'But Rachel, I haven't seen a single bat in the entire time I've spent in Shallow Bay so I'm assuming we might be safe this afternoon. Come and play.'

Play. The idea was so foreign to her that it scared her.

'You might even want to take that shirt off,' he said and that was more than enough. She'd worn her swimsuit to the beach, with a shirt over the top. After all, she was here in care capacity. Beach lifesaver.

She could still be a beach lifesaver with this shirt on, though, and she could also stand in the shallows and watch the kids throwing plastic surfboards. Tom had seen her scars once. She had no intention of exposing them again.

'The boys probably won't even notice,' he told her, still watching her face. 'Or if they do then it's a ten-second explanation that they're old scars, the same as Kit will have on his hand, and it's done and dusted. Rachel, once they see them once, you won't have to hide any more.'

'But I need to hide.' It was out before she even thought about it. A sweeping statement. A statement that covered her whole life? The words hung in the stillness like an upraised sword, threatening. Stupid, stupid, stupid. What was it with this man that made her feel so exposed?

And his eyes were still on hers, holding. Understanding? How could he understand?

'Rachel, you don't need to do any such thing,' he said. 'You're far too beautiful to hide for the rest of your life. It's time to have fun.' And, before she knew what he was about, he reached down and took her hands, tugging her to her feet.

And once she stood, he didn't let go.

What was happening? She stood facing him, her hands in his, and the wash of vulnerability that hit her was so overwhelming she almost needed his hands to hold her up.

But she didn't need his hands. She didn't need anything. She had to leave.

'I need to go home,' she stammered.

'Liar,' he said. 'You weren't exactly packing up when I arrived.'

'That was because I thought you still needed to sleep. I thought you needed me to be here.'

'I still need you.'

'No!' It was almost panic. 'You don't.'

'I do,' he said placatingly. 'But not in a way that threatens you. I need you to see me whup Marcus in the…what did you say?…the Wipe-Out Wally, Tip-Off Tony and Grommet Georgie competition. I need an audience for my prowess and you're elected. You can keep your shirt on, Dr Tilding. This isn't scary. You might even enjoy yourself.'

'I don't…'

'Enjoy yourself. I can see that and that's why I'm asking. You prescribed me rest this afternoon because I needed it so now I'm returning the favour. Fun, Dr Tilding. You might even have a go, too. Let's see if the boys will share.'

Share… For some reason the word sounded terrifying.

But he was tugging her down to the water and she didn't have a choice.

Tom was intent on having fun, and it seemed Rachel Tilding had to follow.

How seldom was it that Tom Lavery enjoyed himself nowadays? Really enjoyed himself, without the constant niggles of worry that continued to surface?

Answer—hardly ever.

He used to, he conceded. When Claire was well, he'd immersed himself in the role of best buddy to these kids. But when he'd collected the boys for an afternoon's soccer, she'd been waiting at home, ready to take over the moment he was called back to the hospital, or when the demands of his social life took over. He'd enjoyed his time with the boys with no strings. He'd been a joyful pseudo uncle, immersing himself in their fun and laughter, indulging as he liked and then handing them back at will.

He'd lost that, almost the moment Claire had collapsed at work. Sure, he still messed around with them, played with them, but there was always the overriding knowledge that the buck ended with him. If there was a problem, he couldn't mention it to Claire as he was handing them back. He had to fix it himself.

So now…he couldn't play until Claire rang— 'Tom, it's school tomorrow. Are you feeding them junk food? They'll be hyped and it'll be impossible to get them to sleep. Get them home.' Now, he had to judge for himself. Now, he had to face the consequences.

But not this afternoon.

Not with Rachel.

He was rested. He'd organised spaghetti for dinner. Who knew that deciding on what meal came next was such a drag? But, with the afternoon free, he'd sorted it before he'd gone to sleep. Now there was no pressure. The boys were delighted to see him. The competition to see which surfer dude would ride the longest was intense— and Rachel was right there to help.

She was a noticer. He'd had to practically haul her to the water's edge but, once she'd committed, once Henry had handed over Wipe-Out Wally and asked her—tentatively—if she could throw it for him—she'd waded right in. Tom's role turned out to be helping Kit throw Tip-Off Tony. Rachel's first toss went further than his.

The boys whooped with excitement and the challenge was on.

But, no matter how much she was immersed in their fun, he saw Rachel constantly monitoring the kids, watching their expressions, seeing that no one was feeling left out. When Henry started to droop, she put Wipe-Out Wally into his hands, lifted him up and carted him waist-deep so he could throw it even further. Tom, who'd worn trousers to the beach—how dumb was that?—was stuck in the shallows. Kit and Marcus headed out too, so it was game on between the four of them, with Tom watching from the sidelines.

Rachel might be whooping with the kids, but still he saw that watchfulness. The care to shield Kit's hand, to edge around Kit so Marcus's wild swings didn't make contact.

He thought of her as she wanted to be, a radiologist isolated in her technical world, not needing to interact, and he thought, What a waste.

She was lit up, vivacious, laughing, her reserve set aside, and she fascinated him. Her shirt was clinging to her body, hiding the scars. They were still there, but hidden.

Surface scars. He was watching her now, fascinated by the woman underneath.

She was gorgeous. Strong, feisty, caring...

Not caring. She wouldn't define it as such, he thought. She'd define it as accepting responsibility but as he watched her watching the boys, making sure each was safe and having fun, he thought she had the definition wrong. She just had to see it.

Could he show her what caring really was? Could he find the Rachel underneath the prickles? Underneath the wounds?

The memory of last night's kiss was suddenly all around him. He watched her hold Henry and jump a wave and he thought, She truly is beautiful.

But what was he thinking? A wave splashed up, foam spraying high, and the dose of cold water was what he needed.

He was standing behind three needy kids whose care was in his hands. Back on the shore was Tuffy, a rescue dog who'd been on death row when he and the boys had gone to the shelter to find a cute pup and brought home a three-legged, undernourished mutt instead.

Four rescued souls. But they helped each other,

he thought. The boys had each other, and that made them far more independent than if he'd been landed with only one.

And Tuffy? Yes, he'd been rescued, but Tom had watched each of the boys form their own attachment to the little dog. Especially Henry, who had had nightmares ever since Claire's death. Tom's method of dealing with them was to wake him, hug him and then pop a very willing Tuffy into bed with him, and there were many times when each boy was comforted with individual Tuffy-cuddles.

There were still times when the combined needs of three small boys were too much for Tom, with or without Tuffy. But Tuffy had helped. Adding another 'rescue' had eased the situation, not added to it.

All this was floating as an uneasy, nebulous idea while he watched Rachel turn her back to a wave so Henry wouldn't get splashed, and then check immediately that the wave hadn't knocked either Marcus or Kit over.

If he could get through that shell…

He had to be kidding.

The reality of what his stupid, overtired mind was suggesting slammed home. Dad and three kids and dog, with mum to close the circle? Happy families?

This was nuts.

'Where's a wet fish when I need a good slap across the face?' he said out loud. No one heard him. They were having too much fun. All of them.

Family. Rachel?

He definitely needed a wet fish. A big one. He'd known her for a week. She was here out of necessity, not desire. She was scarred, in more ways than one. Her career path was set in stone and it surely didn't include Shallow Bay and a guy lumbered with three kids and a dog. And as for him…he had enough on his plate without being saddled with her baggage.

But the way she'd felt last night…

Then a wave, bigger than the rest, crested and broke straight over them. Marcus yelped and jumped and managed to avoid going under. Rachel jumped too, with Henry scooped up in front of her, but Kit wasn't so lucky. He was slapped hard and disappeared under the foam.

Tom was surging into the surf before he knew it, heading for where he'd last seen Kit, but Rachel was quicker than him. She still held Henry but with her other arm she scooped up Kit and tucked him firmly against her.

She was soaked. Her curls were clinging every which way. Her arms were full of kids. Marcus edged towards her and somehow she made contact with him too.

'Wipe-out,' she said matter-of-factly as Tom reached her and relieved her of Kit. 'I got us, even if we're all soggy. But look, guys, our little surfers are almost reaching the picnic basket. Look at them go!'

And she had their attention. The three little surfer figures, caught by the bigger than usual wave, were still cruising in, doing just what they were designed to do.

'They'll reach our picnic,' Henry breathed, forgetting about the wave. 'But mine'll get there first.'

'No, it's Kit's who's winning,' Rachel decreed as the wave surged over the dry sand. The tide was coming in fast and the picnic basket was definitely at risk. 'Tip-Off Tony's reached the furthest. In the interest of saving what's left of the cupcakes, I declare the competition officially closed. So Kit gets the pick of the medals I made specially. You want to see them?'

Of course they did. Of course Tom did.

'They're in a bag in the bottom of the picnic basket,' Rachel told them.

Trauma forgotten, Kit wriggled from Rachel's arms and headed for shore. Tom watched with something akin to disbelief.

Was this the same woman who'd spent her first weekend here tidying to the point of compulsion? She was sodden. She'd lifted kids he could hardly believe she could carry. The water had helped, of course, but even so, the combined weight of Kit and Henry had probably been that of a decent adult. She was now watching them run up the beach, seemingly oblivious to the fact that water was still dripping down her face. That other waves were rolling in. That she was being buffeted by the sea.

Another wave hit and she rocked with it. He reached out to steady her but suddenly reality seemed to sink home. She'd been watching the kids and smiling but as his arm touched her she backed off, even as it meant she copped the full force of the wave.

'I'm okay,' she told him brusquely. 'But look at you. You're soaked.'

'You and me both.'

'Yeah, but I'm dressed for it.' She turned and looked out to sea at a boat chugging past, but he was aware that she was doing it to break contact between them. 'The fishing boat out there,' she said, and he heard a note of guilt. 'I saw it come past. I should have known it'd cause a surge.'

'It was hardly dangerous when you were so close.'

'I should have been closer. They were only out this deep because I was with them. I shouldn't have let them...'

'You were having fun,' he said gently. 'And so were they. They're safe and they're happy. That's all that matters.'

The boys were back at the basket now. Tom saw them raise three huge medallion-type circles on scarlet ribbon.

'They say "Super Surfer One", "Ace Surfer Two" and "Surfer Spectacular Three",' Kit shouted. 'I'm Super Surfer One!' He put the medallion round his neck and whooped off along the beach, his brothers whooping after.

'Where did you get those?' Tom asked faintly, watching three little boys, each with a medal thumping across his chest.

'A cornflake packet, Texta pen and gift wrap

ribbon,' she said. 'I thought I might need something to finish the afternoon with. Organised R Us.'

'Where did you learn…?'

'I had a great foster mother,' she told him. 'Once. Briefly.'

'You're amazing.'

'No, I'm just organised. I think of all eventualities.'

'Because you've had to.'

'Let's not go there,' she told him brusquely, and then she shivered. 'I'm getting cold. Time to go home.'

Home.

Two homes.

One, Rachel's little cottage.

Two, his, where chaos reigned.

'We have spaghetti at our place,' he told her. 'Feel like sharing?'

'Why would I want to?'

It was a strange answer, harsh, an instinctive response rather than a thought-out one. She heard it and corrected herself almost instantly. 'Sorry. That wasn't very gracious. Thank you for the offer but no, I have work to do.'

'More lyssavirus study?'

'You never know when those bats will strike,' she said, and he heard the effort she made to keep her voice light. 'So, moving on, Dr Lavery...' She shivered again.

Once again he had an almost irresistible urge to reach out to her, but he knew what her response would be. He could see it.

He could see fear.

This afternoon he'd needed her and she'd responded with generosity and thoughtfulness. Now, though, the need was over and she was withdrawing.

But he... He still needed?

That was a crazy thought.

She was moving on. He could only watch as she headed up the beach, grabbed a towel and started rubbing the water from her curls.

He wanted to help.

No, he didn't. If he started feeling like that, it'd make matters very messy.

Except he was feeling like that.

And suddenly Dr Tom Lavery was starting to see a plan. Right now it was no more than a thought bubble, but it wasn't to be rejected out of hand. There was time to see if it was feasible. Two years of time.

It did seem nuts, but the idea had lodged and wouldn't go away.

He'd need patience. He'd need luck and he'd need to be a lot surer than he was now. But the more he thought about it... He'd rescued three kids and a dog already. Was it even vaguely possible that one gorgeous, feisty, defensive woman could complete the picture for them all?

She headed back to her cottage, feeling weird.

She shouldn't. She'd acted according to need, which was her mantra. Do what was needed in order to survive. In order to get on. In order to make the people around her be nice to her.

Hadn't she learned that the hard way? Placate and placate and placate, in the hope that conflict could be avoided.

There hadn't been the threat of conflict this afternoon, but there'd been concern about an exhausted colleague. She'd accepted responsibility. She'd sorted it. She should feel okay.

So why was she feeling weird? Why was she feeling as if she'd rather have stayed on the beach for a while, maybe headed back to have dinner with them? Be part of what they were?

That was the age-old yearning, she told herself.

Rachel Tilding, on the outside looking in. Tom was somehow creating his version of happy families, and hadn't she learned the hard way what happened when you did that? Foster families had folded under the strain of having her associated baggage. Events had just…happened…leaving her more desolate than when she'd started.

Like her, Tom had acted according to need, she conceded, but he'd had no choice. He had to be where fate had placed him, but she had a choice. She'd made it years ago when she'd walked out of her last foster home and closed the door behind her.

She walked back into her little cottage and once again the door closed behind her.

Leaving Tom and his scary version of happy families firmly on the other side.

# CHAPTER EIGHT

LIFE SETTLED DOWN to how it ought to be. How she'd expected it to be. She was working to the best of her ability before she returned to the nice anonymous city where she could get on with her future career.

There'd been a period after her afternoon with the boys where she'd felt unsettled. As if life was teetering towards something she couldn't control. The next time she'd seen Tom he'd smiled at her in a way she'd found disturbing, his eyes full of warmth and laughter. He'd told her the boys were looking forward to a repeat.

'Only in an emergency,' she'd said, more harshly than she'd intended.

'Why? Didn't you have fun?'

'They enjoyed themselves. That's all that matters.'

And that was that. She had no intention of taking anything further.

With one month down—only one year and

eleven months to go!—she had reason to feel satisfied. She hadn't seen her first case of lyssavirus, but she was learning more about family medicine every day. Even the medical needs of the valley seemed to have settled. Col was back on his farm, on his beautifully repaired hip. Roscoe's son was thriving. Frances Ludeman had successfully delivered her sixth baby and declared that was the end of it.

'I need to feel like I have some control over my life,' she'd told Rachel. Rachel wondered how on earth having six children equated with control, but she could agree with the sentiment.

Control was what Rachel valued at all costs, and if she had to ignore the weird way Tom Lavery's smile made her feel…well, that was a small cost for keeping her world safe.

'You want to come to a birthday party?'

It was Monday morning. Rachel had just completed a ward round. Tom was due to run the clinic while Rachel was scheduled for vaccinations at the local library.

'We don't bring the babies into the clinic for vaccinations,' Tom had told her. 'There's an increased risk of catching bugs brought in by sickies, and besides, we don't want kids' first experience of clinic to be a needle. The library puts on morning tea. It has a toy section. Apart from a tiny prick, the parents enjoy it, and so do the kids.'

It wasn't as efficient, Rachel had thought as he'd told her, but then there was a lot that wasn't efficient in family medicine.

One year, eleven months…

'A birthday?' she said now, cautiously, and he smiled. Drat it, she wished he wouldn't. He was a colleague and why that smile twisted something that had no right to be twisted…

'Kit's birthday,' he told her. 'Saturday afternoon. Mostly in the garden if it's good weather, or in my living room—heaven help me—if it's not. Anybody who's anybody will be there—twelve kids at least—and Kit says he'd love you to come.'

'Kit scarcely knows me.'

'That's not true. He thinks of you as a friend.'

'How can I be a friend? I'm not.'

'Really?' He eyed her cautiously. 'So what makes a friend, Rachel Tilding?'

'I…'

'Is it someone who helps out in times of trouble?' He answered himself. 'That's a decent definition and you're a fine fit.'

'I do what I have to do,' she said a bit crossly, trying to avoid his gaze. Those eyes. 'I'll cover you medically, make sure Kit's party isn't interrupted.'

'Saturday afternoon's normally quiet. Can I tell Kit you'll come?'

He raised his brows in question, and his eyes still held hers. Smiling. There was understanding behind that smile, and it got to her.

He thought she was afraid?

She wasn't. Okay. A birthday party. Lots of people. She could pop in and out, get it out of the way.

'Fine,' she snapped, and then caught herself. There was no need to snap. This was a child's birthday party, nothing to be angry about. 'I'll make cupcakes.'

He grinned at that. 'That would be excellent, though actually I have a favour to ask. You did say you liked cooking?'

'I do.'

'Then how about a birthday cake? I was going to order one from the bakery, but the choice is pink or blue butter cakes and even I think they're a bit ordinary.'

She relaxed. This was something easy, even enjoyable. It was also a reason she could tell herself she was going. She could put it in her 'accept responsibility' basket.

'I'd enjoy making a birthday cake,' she told him and was rewarded by a smile that seemed almost blinding. That had her taking an instinctive step back.

'Thank you,' he told her. 'Two p.m. on Saturday.'

'Tom…' She was fighting against that smile. Fighting to get herself back in control. Back to medicine, fast. 'Lois Manning… You know her? Her husband, Bob, was here with a cow kick when I first arrived. I admitted her yesterday with a chest infection. Her blood pressure's up, but not to worrying levels. X-ray shows a couple of minor suspect areas—still not enough to worry about, but I thought a night on IV antibiotics and a bit of enforced bed rest might clear things faster. But she's not settling. The next step seems to be an ambulance trip over to Ferndale for a CT scan, but the idea seems to be distressing her even more. Maybe you could pop in and reassure her?'

Which was sensible.

One of the things she'd learned in the last month was the power of Tom Lavery. It wasn't just the almost irresistible combination of his smile, his gentle bedside manner and his skill, though they carried weight with the locals—and with Rachel. It was the fact that Tom was the grandson of the old doctor. The community gave him a level of trust that she doubted she'd ever achieve. If this was to be her lifetime career maybe she'd try, but she was here as a temporary doctor. If the patients required trust, then she was sensible enough to call on Tom.

'Let's see her together,' Tom told her. 'You're her treating doctor. Let's put me where I belong, simply a second opinion before we go to the expense and trouble of a transfer.'

'Thank you,' she said, steadying as she retreated to work mode. Back to practicalities. 'Now?'

'Why not?' he said and glanced at his watch. 'Clinic for me and vaccinations for you. Both starting at nine, which is in ten minutes. Which means we're both already running late.'

'Then there's no need for me to come with you.'

'There is a need. We do this together,' Tom told her. 'If I'm seen as overriding you, then my workload will increase tenfold. I have to be seen as trusting you. Which I do. Absolutely. After you, Dr Tilding.'

And what was there in that to make her colour rise? She felt her cheeks flush with the compliment—with the warmth in his words—and then with the way he put his palm fleetingly against the small of her back as she entered Lois's room.

It was just as well he was behind her. There was no reason for her to blush, and no way she wanted him to see he had that power.

But then she was in Lois's room. Lois was turned away from her in the bed and Rachel's dumb reactions were put aside. Even from the door she could see Lois was sobbing.

Why was she so frightened? She thought of what she'd said to her. On the basis of pain and trouble with breathing she'd suspected there might be a pneumonia which would need immediate treatment, but she'd suspected nothing worse.

'Lois, there's no need to be frightened,' she told her, speaking quickly. 'The trip across to Ferndale is merely a precaution. I'm almost certain they'll send you straight back.'

'I know that.' Lois was a tall, gaunt woman in her late sixties, her face weathered from a life spent on the farm. She'd come across as sensible, but as well as an obvious chest infection Rachel had noticed trembling hands and a slight fever. She'd thought maybe fatigue was playing a part, which was the real reason she'd kept her in overnight. She'd been disappointed and mildly surprised when the symptoms had escalated.

'Lois, would you mind if I listen to your chest before you go?' Tom perched on the end of the bed and smiled reassuringly at her. 'Dr Rachel's already listened and she's not too worried. Can I listen in as well?' He hauled his stethoscope out of his pocket and leaned forward. It was an informal way of conducting an examination—doctor sitting on bed. Any old-fashioned head nurse would have a stroke at the sight of all those neat hospital corners messed up, Rachel thought, but Tom was nothing if not informal.

He listened and Rachel found a wad of tissues and Lois mopped her eyes and tried to look more cheerful. And failed.

'Your chest doesn't sound too bad,' Tom said when he'd had a decent listen and made Lois cough. 'A bit raspy but nothing a simple infection can't explain. How long have you been crook?'

'Three days. Maybe less. But yesterday… Bob was worrying. And maybe I got scared.' It was a tremulous whisper.

'So what's scaring you?' Tom asked bluntly. 'Are you thinking you have lung cancer?'

That took Rachel aback, but she watched Lois's face and she knew it had been the elephant in the room, an unspoken fear.

'Yes,' Lois whispered.

'But the cough only started three days ago.'

'Y-yes.'

'Lung cancer doesn't usually move so fast,' Tom told her. 'It's likely that you've copped a simple infection which will respond well to what we're doing. A CT scan will check more thoroughly. Patterns of shadowing can identify areas of infection and suggest which bug's causing the problem. If it's anything out of left field a CT will let us nip that in the bud early. And yes, it'll also show a cancer if there is one, but Lois, I'd eat my fishing hat if we found cancer, and I'm very fond of my fishing hat.'

Lois gave a watery chuckle, sniffed and blew her nose. 'I…thank you. I know. It's sensible.'

'So how's Bob doing?' Tom asked, settling back on the bed as if he was here for the long haul. Rachel frowned and glanced at her watch. There was no need to make themselves even later by stopping for a chat.

'He's good.'

'His leg's cleared up? That was some kick he got.'

'Jerseys,' Lois said with disdain. 'We run organic now. It's the only way to make money from such a small farm, and Jersey milk is the best seller, but they're bast—hard cows to manage.'

'I've met one or two Jerseys in my time,' Tom told her. 'Grandpa ran them as house cows before Gran got fed up and made him swap to Friesians.' Then he added, almost casually, 'And your daughter? Sandra, isn't it? How's she doing?'

And Lois's face crumpled again. She sobbed into her tissues and Tom sat and waited as if he had all the time in the world.

This was nothing to do with her, Rachel

thought. It was nothing to do with medicine. She should edge out and head off for her vaccinations. But there was something about this tableau that had captured her. Tom looked totally relaxed. Casual. Somehow, he'd turned this into what seemed almost a fireside chat with a friend, instead of a consultation with a patient.

How did he do that? And what was the point?

He was acting as if he had all the time in the world. All the patience.

She felt as if she was in some sort of masterclass, seeing something she had no hope of replicating.

'Sandra's in a refuge,' Lois said at last, gulping, trying hard not to cry. 'One of those women's refuges. With the kids. The police… Stuart broke her arm, trashed the place. Her oldest—Will—he's got a really deep cut over his eye and bruises where his dad kicked him. The neighbours came. They got her and the kids away. Stuart got arrested but she thinks he's out on bail. He busted her phone, but she rang from the refuge—they let her use their phone. She says… she says she's okay, but we know she's not. Bob's trying to send her money but she's not game to even go out of the refuge to buy anything. And we want her to come here but there's something to do with the kids' passports and Stuart's permission, and she doesn't even know where the passports are because of the mess the house is in. She'd never be game to go back and search. And Bob and I need to go to her but there's the cows and we need the money to bring her and the kids over. And...'

And she subsided into her tissues again.

Leaving Rachel aghast. Shortness of breath and high blood pressure were symptoms of an infection, but how could they possibly improve with this behind them?

She should have asked. Why hadn't she asked?

She hadn't even known Lois had a daughter.

She did, though, she realised. Tom had told her when Bob was ill. And even if she hadn't realised, maybe she should have probed before heading straight to expensive scans.

She felt very junior, and very small.

'Right,' Tom said, sounding now very much like a consultant who'd figured the diagnosis and was prescribing treatment he was sure of. 'How long since you've talked to Sandra?'

'Yesterday.' Lois's voice quavered. 'She doesn't like to use their phone.'

'Then we can fix that. As a doctor, I can access links that'll let us contact the refuge. Not directly. There'll be all sorts of precautions in place to keep Sandra safe, but indirectly... If we go through the proper channels I'm thinking we could get her a computer-type notepad—a tablet—with internet hooked up. Do you use the internet?'

'Bob does.' Lois sounded confused. 'We have a computer at home he uses for bills and such. But it's old.'

'Let's get you a tablet, too,' Tom said. 'You know my grandpa set up an endowment for the hospital? This is just the sort of thing he wanted it used for.'

'I can't...' Lois breathed.

'You don't have to. Grandpa already did. So what's next? I'm going to ask Jenny's lad, Lachlan, to give you a lesson on how to use it. You know Lachie? He broke his hip rock-climbing a couple of weeks ago. He's wheelchair-bound, home from uni and bored stupid. I'll ring the techie store over at Ferndale and get them to put your notebook on the bus this morning and we'll see if we can get one to Sandra just as fast. Because it's a police case, I reckon I can use their

Social Welfare unit to help Sandra. With Lachie's help and a bit of luck you'll be video-calling by dinner time.'

'Video-calling?'

'It's like telly,' he said, smiling confidently at her stunned expression. 'Looking at each other's face on the screen while you're talking. It's the next best thing to being with her. You can almost give her a virtual hug, and you'll be able to talk to each other all day if you want.'

He paused, thinking it through, but then forged ahead with the next thing. 'Next is the kids' passports and exit permissions. New Zealand and Australia are so close and there's good communication at high level. Have there been problems with Stuart before?'

'Lots,' Lois told him.

'Anything documented?'

'He hurt her badly last year.' Lois still sounded stunned. 'He ended up hitting one of the neighbours and the police were called. Sandra wouldn't press charges—she never does—but the neighbour did. Stuart got off with a suspended sentence or something. Sandra went back to him, of course. She says it's her fault, she annoys him.

Over and over she says it; he has her too sub-
dued to think about fighting. But this time he
hit William and he's only seven. Will tried to
stop him hitting Sandra and he turned on him.
Surely she can't go back to him now.' She broke
off and hiccupped another sob.

But Tom was nodding as if all was going to
plan. 'Lois, this is excellent,' he said. 'Let's not
think about the past. Let's focus on the future.
So Stuart has a previous conviction for domes-
tic violence. I'm sure we can use that. I have an
old uni friend who's now a lawyer in Canberra,
something high up in immigration. I lent him my
dinner suit when I was nineteen—for his first
date with a girl he was keen on. But apparently
my suit was left on the bedroom floor, and before
he could give it back his girlfriend's Labrador
had puppies on it. He couldn't afford to buy me
a new one. Over time I suspect he's forgotten,
and I haven't called in the debt. I believe this is
the time to remind him.'

He smiled, cheerfulness and optimism per-
sonified. 'So who knew puppies could be use-
ful? For such a favour—I reckon he even owes

me his marriage!—we might have Sandra and the kids helping milk your cows by Monday.'

Lois was looking even more stupefied than Rachel felt. 'You're serious?'

'Never more so. You know what? If Dr Rachel concurs, we might leave the trip across to Ferndale in favour of video-calling lessons instead. But for now...' He checked his watch. 'I really need to get things moving if I'm to get that tablet on the Ferndale bus. Let's get some details and then I want you to snuggle down and sleep until we have something concrete to tell you. Is that okay with you?'

'That's...that's fine,' Lois murmured, sounding totally bewildered.

Tom rose—and then, to Rachel's astonishment, he leaned over the gaunt woman in the bed and gave her a solid, reassuring hug. Then, still holding her, he forced her to meet his gaze.

'Lois, we'll do our best to fix this,' he told her. 'This is not all on your shoulders. We're calling in the big guns while you sleep. But sleep you will and that's an order. Do you concur, Dr Tilding?'

'I concur,' she said faintly.

'Excellent,' he said and beamed. 'There is still

the matter of a mucky chest but the antibiotics might take advantage of sleep to get on with their work. I do like a definitive course of action.'

'Lovely,' Lois murmured and grasped his hand. 'You're lovely.'

'I need to go,' Rachel said shakily. 'I have vaccinations waiting. Excuse me.'

And she fled.

He'd seen her face as she'd left, and even though they were both late he suspected she wouldn't head straight to her vaccination appointments. He'd seen her before on the back veranda, taking a quick breather between patients, and that was where he found her.

It was the same place they'd kissed the night of Col's operation. Then, though, there'd been mutual relief at a great outcome. Now Rachel's hands were pressed to her cheeks. She looked a picture of mortification.

'Rachel?'

'How did I do that?' she whispered. 'Missed diagnosis. Argh! If you hadn't intervened she'd be in the ambulance, getting more stressed over tests she doesn't need.'

'Hey, you weren't to know.'

'I should have asked.'

'About a daughter you hadn't heard of?'

'I had heard of her. You told me when Bob was sick.'

'I tell you heaps of things about the locals. So does Roscoe, and so does Jenny, and probably half the population of Shallow Bay. You can't be expected to remember all of it. Besides, she may still be sitting on pneumonia.'

'We both know it's unlikely. Shallow breathing, chest pain, fear... The only symptom not explained by anxiety is the fever, and even that was slight.'

'And there were shadows on her X-ray.'

'Marginal.'

'So you're beating yourself up why?'

'Because I didn't get it.' The sun was glinting on the sea below them but she wasn't noticing the view. 'It's not just that I didn't get it. It's that I *don't* get it. I don't read the signs. That's why I should be starting radiology right now instead of pretending to be a family doctor. You read Lois right off. Me, I floundered. I'm a medical technician. I join the dots I can see, but when the dots are emotional they're invisible. It's like I'm colour blind.'

'But you're learning,' he said gently. 'I've watched you. You care.'

'I don't care,' she said, almost wildly. 'I don't know how to. I've just learned to follow the rules.'

'You're saying you don't feel emotion?'

'I *can't* feel emotion. It scares me.'

'There's nothing to be scared of.'

'Of course there is. How can you doubt it? It gets you into all sorts of trouble. Like hugging a patient with an infection. Cross contamination? Why would you do that? And ethics? Hugging? That's the biggie. You must have attended the lectures on medical defence. You know the boundaries.'

'Well, contamination's hardly a problem,' he said dryly. 'Or I can't let it be. Do you know how many people sneeze at me every day? One hug is hardly likely to make a difference. And I didn't cross any ethical boundaries with Lois.'

'That's not what Medical Defence would say.'

'What, hugging a patient to comfort her, to say she's not in this alone? How is that ethically wrong? I even had a female colleague there as chaperone—you—but it wouldn't have mattered if I hadn't. Do you think she could possibly take it the wrong way?'

'I'd never risk it. I don't touch. Ever.'

'Really?' He looked at her with concern, seeing her internal struggle. He was starting to figure her out by now. So much had been hammered out of her by her awful childhood, by adults who'd betrayed her in the worst way—but there was so much still in there. He wanted to reach out and hug her, and it was an almost physical struggle not to.

But the more he saw of Rachel Tilding, the more he knew he had to try. And it wasn't just sympathy, he acknowledged. She made him feel...

Yeah, well, he couldn't go there. It was enough for the moment to accept that he had to get through those barriers.

'So...the night of Col's operation,' he said slowly. 'You touched me then. Was that comfort, or was that something else?'

And, rightly or wrongly, things suddenly moved to a whole new level. He watched Rachel's face and saw confusion. And panic.

She was remembering that kiss.

'You know that wasn't comfort,' she managed.

'You're right—it was something else. It was stupid.'

'It didn't feel stupid,' he said, and he could resist the confusion, the fear, on her face no longer. He reached out and took her hands. Gently though. She could pull away if she wished. 'But no, it wasn't comfort. Maybe it started that way but that kiss, Rachel, was something else entirely.'

'It wasn't. I mean…' She seemed to be struggling with words, struggling with the feel of her hands in his. Struggling with the urge to pull away?

She could if she wanted to, he thought, but her body didn't seem to be cooperating.

'Do you get the difference between comfort and what's happening between us?' Tom asked. The link between them felt warm. Strong. Right. 'Rachel, you need to forget the fear. Leave it in the past, where it belongs. Here are people you can trust.'

He hesitated for a moment, fighting to gather his thoughts, but then he forged on. 'Rachel, you're with a community now, with people you could learn to love and who could learn to love you. A lot of people. And, to be honest, I want to be included in that mix. I know this sounds dumb, but for the last month every time I turn a corner and see you I feel myself breaking into a smile. There's this thing between us. I think...'

'Then don't think,' she snapped, panic-stricken. 'And don't say it.' But still she didn't pull away.

'Don't say what?'

'That you care.'

'Why not?'

'Because there's no way I can care back.'

But the link of her hands sent a different message. The panic on her face... She was so torn.

'You can learn to care,' he said, steadily now. 'Like I've learned to care—deeply—for three kids. Like I've learned to care for one three-legged dog. Like I'm learning to care for this whole damned valley. I didn't ask to come here, Rachel. Left to my own devices, I'd be a practising orthopaedic surgeon, dating who I liked and surfing on the side. But here I am, in Shallow Bay doing what I can. Caring. And as for you... Rachel, you're beautiful, talented and you care as well. You wouldn't be distressed now if you didn't care.'

'I accept responsibility when I need to. That's not caring.'

'So the kiss between us was…responsible?'

'No!'

'So what was it?' His voice became even more gentle. 'Why the fear?'

'I'm not afraid.'

'I think you are.'

'Well, I'm not,' she said, struggling to sound cross rather than panicked. 'You have tickets on yourself if you think one kiss from you and I'm thrown for a hoop.'

'Tickets on myself?'

'Tom, this whole situation is inappropriate. We have work to do. We should not be standing on the hospital veranda holding hands, analysing a kiss that should never have happened. If you think that it was so important…yes, you have tickets on yourself. The conceit of the male race knows no bounds, you definitely included. Now, can I get on with my work?'

'If you can prove that one kiss means nothing.'

'It doesn't!'

'So…'

'Tom…'

'Okay.' He released her hands and held up his—surrender. 'I'm conceited enough to think that kiss *was* something more. But I'm excused because I'm admitting that one kiss…as you say…threw *me* for a hoop. Me, not you. Or was it both of us? Was it indeed an aberration? Okay, Dr Tilding, let's take this as a clinical trial. One more kiss to find out?'

'You can't be serious. How unprofessional is this?'

'A clinical trial's professional,' he protested. 'Compared to hugging patients… According to your rules I should be struck off every medical register in the country. So…one kiss, Rachel Tilding. Prove to me it meant nothing.'

'It did. I can't.'

'Why not?'

'Vaccinations,' she said wildly. 'Clinic. I'm late…'

'Rachel…' He grinned, putting his finger on her lips to shush her. 'One thing Shallow Bay knows is that our medical service works on a triage system. Priorities are allocated according to need. So right now you're looking at me with something maybe neither of us understand but it's something we need to diagnose. That need for diagnosis puts you—and me—right up the top of the list.'

'No! Tom, I don't want it.'

'Really?' He cupped her chin with his fingers, looking down into her confused eyes. Her panicked eyes. Maybe he should walk away, but he couldn't leave her like this.

He couldn't leave her.

'You really don't want me to kiss you?' he said gently. 'Really?'

'I...'

'Say it, Rachel. Say you don't want me to kiss you.'

'No...yes...no...'

'Decide, Rachel,' he said almost sternly. 'Say it.'

She looked so confused. Well, so was he, he admitted. He had no idea where this was going.

And this place was hardly private. A hospital veranda, mid-morning. Any minute now, nursing staff, patients, visitors could walk by. This was crazy.

So why did this feel like the most important moment of his life?

'Yes or no, Rachel?' he said, and he looked down into her gorgeous eyes and saw her panic and he saw her confusion, but he also saw... something else.

His hands were cupping her face, tilting her mouth. She was so close. So lovely.

This was crazy. He shouldn't...

'Yes,' she whispered—and then there was no need for words for a very long time.

She was mad. Utterly, incomprehensibly mad.

She'd let Tom kiss her and she'd kissed him back. Again!

She had no idea why she'd done it. Hormones, she told herself as she headed to the library to her waiting babies. It was the same hormones that saw fifteen-year-olds get pregnant when pregnancy was the last thing they wanted. Total, idiotic madness.

She wasn't fifteen years old now. The fact that Tom's understanding, his gorgeous smile, his crazy reasoning about clinical trials had broken her defences...

It was definitely hormones and she needed to pull herself together fast.

Once at the library she coped with vaccinations with professional competence. She smiled when she needed to smile. She comforted, she complimented, she gave injections to protect the babies of Shallow Bay from danger.

But why did it seem as if she'd just walked over a cliff herself?

'So...'

Clinic was finished. Tom was sitting in the hospital kitchen wolfing down a sandwich before he headed out on house calls. He was also waiting on phone calls from Canberra and New Zealand, which was the reason he was eating fast, aware that slabs of time would be taken up as soon as these calls came through.

Roscoe had come to find him. The big nurse had taken two weeks' paternity leave after the birth of his son and he was now back at work, looking a little sleep-deprived but also absurdly happy. And wanting to share his happiness with everyone.

'So?' Tom said cautiously between mouthfuls.

'What's happening?'

'With Lois?' He'd given Roscoe a fast explanation before clinic. 'The tablet should be here by now.'

'Yeah, Lachie's in there now, explaining video calls. Bob's there, too. Sandra hasn't received hers yet but it's happening. Meanwhile, they're practising calling my Lizzy. Lizzy's a huge fan of video calls—she uses them all the time to talk to her mum and dad in Sydney. When I left the room, Lois and Bob were being coerced into sharing nappy changing by video link.'

Tom grinned. Great. This was a terrific little community, he thought, and once they had Sandra here the community would protect its own.

'But that's not what my "So" was about,' Roscoe said, and plonked himself down and snagged one of Tom's sandwiches. 'You and Our Rachel.'

'Our Rachel?'

'She's been here over a month. She's therefore one of ours. And Our Poppy swore she saw you snogging out on the veranda this morning. And we both know it's not the first time, don't we, Doc? Anyway, Poppy said it's none of her business and she hates being a gossip, so she managed not to tell anyone for a whole three minutes. Which is huge for Our Poppy.'

And, despite the dismay he felt at being sprung, he had to smile at that. Poppy was Shallow Bay's most junior nurse. She lived and breathed romance, and now she'd seen a real live kiss…

'She has you married and living happily ever

after, and she's already predicting three more kids,' Roscoe said. 'Two girls and another boy. She hasn't named them yet but she's close.' He munched his—Tom's—sandwich and Tom gave up trying.

'A bit premature,' he managed.

'You think?' Roscoe's grin was huge but then it faded. 'Seriously, Doc... You and Rachel...?'

'She feels good to hold,' he said simply, and his friend stared at him.

'You're serious.'

'Hell, Roscoe...'

'She's hardly warm and cuddly,' Roscoe said, obviously thinking it through. He frowned. 'I know, it's none of my business. But who knows what's under that cool surface?'

Tom shrugged, abandoned his sandwiches and gave up any pretence of keeping how he was feeling to himself. 'That's what I intend to find out.'

'You're kidding.' Roscoe even forgot his sandwich. 'Wow, Doc...'

'I know.' He shrugged. 'I'm playing with fire.'

'Yeah, if this goes belly up, we either lose a doctor or we have doctors who won't speak to each other for two years.'

'And if it doesn't go belly up?'

'Doc, she's damaged. Even I can see that.'

'Then we fix it,' he said simply. 'This community...'

'You really are playing with fire.'

'Something has to warm her up,' he said. And then, more seriously, 'And something has to warm me up. Roscoe, I think I need this.'

'Wow,' Roscoe said again and whistled. 'And double and triple wow. Right, then. I have faith. I'll get straight back to Poppy and tell her to start sorting baby names. Two girls and a boy? Let's get this show on the road.'

One semi-public kiss and everyone in Shallow Bay was looking at her sideways. Sometimes not even that. Broad smiles greeted her, and she knew she was being looked at differently. It seemed the population of Shallow Bay was no longer seeing her as a temporary doctor but a long-term solution to what they saw as the gaping hole in Tom's inherited family.

'This isn't fair.'

'What's not fair?' Tom asked. It was Friday afternoon and they were passing in the corridor between patients. She'd been avoiding him all week. Now she had two more patients to see and then Tom was off duty for the weekend. Unless there was an emergency she wouldn't see him. She had promised to attend Kit's birthday party but that could be a quick drop in and run.

Run was the operative word, she decided. This community was driving her nuts. Her last patient had practically offered to do the flowers for her wedding—'I'll give you a great rate'—and everywhere she went there were conspiratorial grins.

She'd had it—and when she turned a corner in the corridor and practically bumped into the cause of the trouble she was ready to vent some spleen.

'How many women have you kissed in the past?' she demanded before he could say a word, and Tom looked taken aback.

'I couldn't say,' he said cautiously. 'Does it matter?'

'It does,' she said crossly. 'You've dated, right?'

'I…yes.'

'Teenage romance? Med school? All those parties as an intern?'

'I had spots in adolescence,' he admitted. 'I was a bit handicapped.'

'I don't care,' she snapped. 'Guesstimate, Tom Lavery. A hundred?'

'Surely not.'

'I bet I'm right, but I'll give you the benefit of the doubt. Let's say eighty-seven. You can adjust it up or down after you've thought about it.'

'Adjust it...where?'

'On the community noticeboard outside the library,' she told him. 'In big, bold lettering. And in the nurses' station. And anywhere else you can think of that might have all the sticky-nosed people of Shallow Bay saying, "Ooh, he kissed Dr Tilding, this means happy-ever-after." I want huge signs saying *Dr Tilding was Kiss Number Eighty-Eight and she doesn't intend to be Eighty-Nine.*'

He grinned, folded his arms and leaned back against the wall. 'What if I'd like you to be Eighty-Nine?'

'Get over it. It's complicating my life.'

'Maybe life's meant to be complicated.'

'Not mine. Tom, back off.'

'I don't want to back off,' he told her. Hospital corridors were definitely not the place for this kind of conversation, but it seemed there was no choice.

'Tom...'

'Rachel, I think I'm falling for you,' he said bluntly. 'And please don't ask me why. Maybe it's your warm and cuddly persona. Maybe it's the way you embrace life...'

'Cut it with the sarcasm.'

'Okay,' he said gently. 'I'll be serious. Maybe it's because I can see underneath that armour you protect yourself with, to the warm, vibrant woman you want to be. All you need is the courage to admit that you can care.'

'No one can give me courage.'

'I expect you're right,' he said, still serious. 'To be honest, I suspect it's already there, used now to keep yourself distant but ready to be used... for life.'

'Tom, you're scaring me.' She had no idea where this was going.

'I don't want to scare you. I want to get to know you.'

'Because you see me as a rescue pet,' she snapped, and watched his brows hike.

'What?'

'You've seen my arms. The moment you saw them things changed. I saw your reaction—so here comes Dr Lavery to the rescue. You helped your friend, Claire, and you rescued her three needy children. You even rescued a dog with three legs. And here I am, damaged as well, a good fit for your houseful of welfare cases.'

'My boys are not welfare cases,' he said, suddenly angry. 'And neither is Tuffy. They just need...'

'They need you. I agree. But I don't.'

'What if I say I need them? And more. What if I need you?'

'Don't be ridiculous. You're the hero. Sadly, I have no taste to be Rapunzel, waiting for rescue.'

'Your hair's too short,' he said, and he tried a smile. She had a sudden, stupid urge to smile back.

He copped a glower instead. 'Tom, please...'

'Could we just relax and enjoy this?' he asked her. 'Could we admit we're attracted to each other and see where it goes?'

'With the whole town watching? We have a quick romantic fling and then I'd be...'

'Left again?' He was watching her face and his eyes told her he was understanding. 'Rachel, there are decent people in the world. People who won't hurt you. People who won't walk away.'

'They won't have the chance,' she told him, totally discombobulated. 'I don't need anyone, including you. Tom, I don't need rescuing. Please, leave me alone. This is scaring me.'

'You like kissing me.'

'Okay, I do, but I don't like what goes with it.'

'What goes with it?' He unfolded his arms and held up his hands, as if in surrender. 'So... Rachel, I know this isn't fair, but will you give me a sop to my pride? Tell me if it wasn't for the boys you'd be all over me like a rash?'

All over him like a rash? What sort of romantic question was that? Weirdly, it broke the tension.

'You're comparing me to measles?'

'In the nicest way.'

'I can see that,' she said. 'But no, the boys have nothing to do with my reaction to you. If you were still a playboy doctor in Sydney I wouldn't be interested, but I bet you wouldn't be interested in me, either.'

'You'd be wrong there.'

She shook her head—and then looked around in relief as Jenny appeared along the corridor, bearing a covered bedpan.

'Clear the path, people,' Jenny said warningly. 'You guys look intense, but old Joe Crazer's enema has finally taken impressive effect.'

Which brought that interlude to a fast end.

Medicine had its uses, Rachel thought as she fled. But Tom's words followed her. Tom's question.

If it wasn't for the boys, would she be all over him like a rash?

No, she thought. In fact, the boys seemed almost a safety net, though they'd got her into trouble in the first place. They'd made her let down her guard. If Tom needed her rather than wanted her then maybe... Maybe.

She wasn't making sense, even to herself. Why would anyone want her? And how could she let herself want Tom? It was all too hard.

What she wanted was to pack her car and head back to the city, away from the prying eyes of a small community, away from a house with a makeshift family next door. Away from the threat Tom posed to her carefully built armour.

How to rebuild her armour?

She'd promised a birthday cake. Tomorrow.

She'd make it, drop it off and run, she decided. But after that...

She was stuck here for two years. How could she cope with that when running seemed the only safe option?

# CHAPTER NINE

THE PARTY WAS scheduled from two to four. The kids had slipped an invitation under her door while she was hunkered down on Friday night, avoiding the world, avoiding even her own thoughts.

There'd be lots of people there. She could do this.

On Saturday morning she rang Tom. 'Do you need the cake before three? I might be late,' she told him. 'Jill Salter won't come in for check-ups and I'm darned if I'll give her another month's insulin without looking at what her sugars are doing. She won't be home until two.'

'That smacks of avoidance.'

'Who? Me? Plan to be late to a party, with noise, sugar, mess? How could you accuse me of such a thing? The cake will be there at three and that's a promise.'

He laughed and let her off the hook, but she disconnected feeling guilty. She could have

been there earlier to help. She could have…been
with him.

*The cake's enough*, she told herself savagely,
and at three o'clock even carrying her cake
across to the house next door felt too much.

The party was in full swing. Twelve children,
Tom had told her, though from the noise it could
have been a hundred.

Tom was in the centre of the back yard, holding a donkey—a huge stuffed toy she recognised as Henry's preferred pillow. They were
playing what was obviously a version of pin-the-
tail. Every child was blindfolded and armed with
strips of fabric. She looked more closely and saw
Velcro glued at the end of each 'tail'.

This was obviously pin-the-tail with a difference. The kids were a tribe with a common goal,
to reach Tom and his donkey and get a tail—any
tail—where it should be.

Working alone, they had no hope. As each
child groped and stumbled and managed to touch
the donkey, Tom chuckled and lifted the donkey
higher, then slipped away.

There were shouts and laughter and tumbles
across the lawn. Tuffy was barking hysterically.
Tom was laughing and scooting and lowering

the donkey so the next kid could just touch—
and then whooping and raising it before scooting again.

Over the heads of the kids Tom's gaze met
hers. His grin was wide and welcoming and the
next kid grabbing for his donkey almost had it.
Tom ducked this time, dropping to all fours with
the donkey tucked under his chest. The kids dis-
integrated into confusion and Rachel found herself grinning.

He was an idiot, she thought. A laughing, loving kid himself.

*Tom.*

'Hey, guys, this isn't working.' It was Marcus,
ever the thoughtful one, yelling from the centre
of the melee. 'We need a trap.'

And while Rachel watched, bemused, Marcus
organised all the kids to one side, their hands
linked. A sweep started across the yard.

Tom had nowhere to go. The line moved in-
exorably. Henry reached him first, grabbed and
yelled. Tom was almost instantly enclosed by
seven small boys and five small girls. The donkey was stuck with random tails and an exhausted, laughing Tom declared the game over.

Blindfolds were removed. The multi-tailed

donkey was paraded around the yard with more whoops but somehow Tom was still looking at Rachel. And she was looking at him.

A great, goofy kid.

A skilled surgeon.

A stepfather.

It was a word she hated but somehow Tom had changed the word for her.

*Tom.*

'Here's the birthday cake, people,' Tom called, still smiling, and the mob descended on her.

'It's a meerkat,' Kit yelled, skidding to a halt in front and staring in stupefaction at his cake.

It was indeed a meerkat. She'd wanted, quite badly, to make it stand tall, gazing in the inquisitive way that made meerkats attract kids the world over. Making an upright meerkat out of chocolate cake, however, had proved beyond her. Instead she'd made him squat, so his back curved in an arch. She'd got his face as she wanted though, peering upward, as if he'd just been disturbed as he foraged in the chocolate/ dust at his feet.

'You'll need to beware bones,' she warned. 'Meerkats have bones.'

'Bones,' Tom said faintly, sounding puffed.

Being pursued as 'donkey' by twelve kids must be something akin to running a marathon.

'Otherwise known as satay sticks,' she told him. 'Every meerkat needs a skeleton.'

'He's awesome,' Kit breathed, and Rachel smiled. It felt okay. More, it felt great to have her splinter skill appreciated. She'd put her all into this meerkat, struggling with satay sticks and chocolate cake and piping bags until the small hours. She reckoned she'd made him pretty realistic—apart from the line of candles along his curved back.

'Too good to eat,' Tom said but the kids looked at him as if he were dumb.

But Kit was looking at the package she had tucked under her arm. A gift. Priorities.

It had arrived two days ago from the States. A T-shirt. A grinning meerkat in Lycra and cape. Personalised.

Across the meerkat's muscled superhero chest was blazoned *Kit Meerkat—Superhero*.

'Kit Meerkat,' Kit stammered and gazed at Tom in awe. 'Can I put it on now?'

'Sure,' Tom said and grinned at Rachel as Kit did the world's fastest quick change.

'There's another gift at the front door,' she told Tom. 'Maybe after cake?'

'You'll stay?'

She hadn't meant to. She'd thought she'd just drop things off and make an excuse.

But Tom was smiling at her and Kit was beaming as if all his Christmases had come at once and two little girls were inspecting her meerkat cake, trying to figure why the head didn't fall off…and suddenly the scene was like a siren song.

It was all the things she avoided. Noise. Chaos. Family?

'Just until after we cut the cake,' she heard herself say. 'Just…to make sure there's no drama with the bones.'

And with that it was decreed it was time to stop for food. Tom hadn't needed her to help him, she realised as they headed into the kitchen. This was a guy's version of a party—piles of bought 'party pies', bowls of cocktail frankfurters, mounds of popcorn and crisps, soda and a huge bowl of watermelon as a nod to being healthy.

Within minutes the table looked as if wolves had descended. Candles were lit. 'Happy Birthday' was sung. Her meerkat was dismembered and devoured—and then Tom reminded them there was something else outside and the pack whooped out into the front garden, leaving chaos behind.

'Go out and I'll clear,' Rachel told Tom, looking at the mess in dismay, but Tom grasped her hand and tugged her out with him.

'Not on your life. We're in this together, Rachel Tilding. If this gift is water pistols, you're in the front line.'

'I'd never do water pistols,' she told him and swallowed a sudden memory of a children's home between foster placements and someone arriving with water pistols and the bullying that followed...

'Rachel?' He was watching her face.

'N-nothing,' she managed. 'Just...ghosts, maybe.'

'Then let's face them together,' he told her. 'Twelve kids hyped on too much excitement and too much sugar, and Rachel Tilding's ghosts. We need to be a team to face this.'

And before she could object he'd tugged her outside.

To where she'd left her birthday gift.

Kit's T-shirt would have been enough of a gift, she conceded, but she hadn't been sure it would arrive in time. She'd ordered this online as well, but from an Australian source. She'd spent an hour wrangling the dodgy pump which came with it. She'd then had to kick it in front of her as she came from next door while carrying the cake, but now the kids were circling what must be the world's biggest beach ball. Almost as high as Henry, all the colours of the rainbow, it bounced and flew whenever it was touched.

And she had plans for it. Once upon a time a foster dad, coping with a tribe of disparate kids, had fashioned this game, and she'd remembered. Now she headed over to the hedge where she'd parked four poles she'd painted the night before. She'd found them in the back shed—tomato stakes. She'd painted two green and two red and attached matching flags. Okay, they were dishcloths, but close enough.

Tom watched, bemused, as she planted green poles at one end of the garden and red poles at the other. 'Right,' she called. 'Two teams. Everyone on this side is on Marcus's team and everyone else is on Kit's. This is Maxi Soccer. Go for it.'

And two minutes later the ball was flying. Kids were flying. The ball was too big and too slippery to grasp. It bounced against kids, against the house, against Rachel and Tom—sometimes even between the posts. Rachel stood on the sidelines and grinned.

'Hey, Dr Smug,' Tom said, his voice full of laughter, and suddenly his hand was holding hers again. 'This is amazing. Well done, you. It's even too light to smash your windows.' He smiled down at her. 'So...no ghosts?'

'They've taken a step back for the duration,' she admitted.

'Kids and family can make that happen,' he told her. They stood side by side, watching the game. Rachel was enjoying the kids' fun. She was also, she conceded, enjoying the sensation of Tom standing right next to her.

She just had to ignore the hormones.

'In a different life I'd ask you out on a date,' he said. They were still watching the game. A bystander would say they were engrossed in what the kids were doing.

They weren't.

'I guess I'd refuse,' she managed.

'Why?'

'Because I don't do relationships.' Flat. Definite. She had the hormones where they needed to be.

'Which is a crazy waste. Rachel, right now you're lonely and isolated and your ghosts are holding sway, but underneath you're a vibrant, loving woman who doesn't deserve to be stuck in a cottage on the other side of the hedge from… life.'

'So you're planning on rescuing me? Like you've rescued three kids and a dog already? Thanks, but I stopped needing rescuing a long time ago.'

'I don't think that's true. But as for rescuing…' He hesitated. 'Okay, I haven't figured it out yet and I always was one for leaping and then looking afterwards. But what I see in you… It makes me realise that rescuing could work both ways.'

'You want me to help rescue you from the kids?'

'I don't need rescuing from the kids,' he told her. 'I love the kids.'

And as if on cue the ball sailed towards him and hit him on the chest with a massive whump. The kids launched themselves after it, and it was all Tom could do to keep standing.

He managed. The ball sailed off to the other side of the garden and they were left alone again.

'Okay, I might need rescuing a bit,' he conceded.

She smiled but she couldn't get the smile to reach her eyes. 'Tom, don't,' she told him. 'Rescue or not... You and me...it's never going to happen. You're missing your career, your life in Sydney, your freedom, the whole life you had before you were lumbered with three kids. I can't help you there.'

'I wasn't lumbered,' he told her. 'I was blessed.'

'I don't believe you. And me... How is rescuing someone else going to help?'

'I won't be rescuing.' His smile deepened. 'Rachel, I'd be loving.'

'Stop! No. What have I ever said to make you think...?'

'You've kissed me,' he said, his smile still lurking. 'Twice so far.'

'Kissing is a huge way from...anything serious.'

'It is, isn't it,' he said, suddenly rueful. 'Rachel, I'm scaring you and that's the last thing I want. Okay. Maybe we should go on a little longer. Maybe not dating because that's hard. Shallow

Bay has a limited number of dating options, to say the least. The Shallow Bay Chippy is hardly dating heaven. But maybe we could add to our occasional kissing total? Seven's a lucky number. When we get to seven...'

'We won't get to seven.'

And then the ball bounced back at them and she saw her chance. Instead of kicking it away, she grabbed it and ran. A muddle of kids surged towards her as she dived towards the goalposts. And scored.

And landed flat on her face.

She lay, winded and stunned. The team she'd scored for roared its approval and the game took off again. Tuffy, though, sat down beside her and licked her face.

The grass was soft. There was no need for Tom to come to her aid. He didn't, for which she was grateful. He stayed watchful, but his smile had gone.

'He looks as stunned as I am,' she told Tuffy, and then she thought, Why wouldn't he be?

'Because propositioning me is ridiculous,' she told Tuffy. 'He's been drinking too much red lemonade.'

The ball was heading her way again. She had to move. Fast. But not towards Tom.

She got up, shook herself off and headed inside. Someone had to clear the mess. Someone had to be practical.

Someone had to keep her armour intact, and that person had to be her.

He'd stuffed it. She'd retreated and he'd had to let her go. He was pushing too hard, for something he hardly understood himself.

At least she'd retreated to his house and not hers, he decided, as parents started arriving to collect their offspring. He handed out party bags and watched the boys wave farewell to their guests and he thought maybe the boys might crash early tonight. Maybe he could take a bottle of wine…

Or not. She had to feel safe in her own house, and heading over after dark with wine…

Back off, he told himself and put a lolly bag into Sophia Lombridge's sticky hand and got a gap-toothed grin in return. Sophia departed, and that was the last of the guests.

Except someone else was coming. A sedan—large, gleaming, black. A model he recognised as being way out of his price range, even when he'd been a surgeon. And as it got closer…

That's all we need, he thought bleakly, for here were Claire's parents. The kids' grandparents. Charles and Marjorie.

He might have known this would happen. He'd endured months of phone calls, increasingly threatening. He'd said they could call the kids whenever they wanted—even though he'd have had to coerce the kids into accepting such calls. He'd suggested he could bring them to Sydney to visit. They were the kids' grandparents and the last thing he wanted was to cut them off completely. But the only thing that would satisfy this pair was custody, and the calls had become threatening.

And then there'd been calls from lawyers. 'It's going to cost you a mint, going down this path, Dr Lavery, and you won't win. Back off now and we can talk about access. If you don't back off you'll end up broke and with no rights at all.'

He'd consulted his own lawyers. He'd dug in. Claire's will had been unequivocal, but the sight of the approaching car made his stomach clench.

The kids saw it too. They left their ball game and came and stood behind him, silent. Scared?

Rachel appeared at the doorway, tea towel in hand. 'Tom, are these glasses yours or do they go back in the boxes?'

But then she saw the approaching car and she froze. Maybe it was the stillness of the kids. Maybe it was his own stillness.

Rachel had been tossed about as a kid as well. She'd have a nose for threats, he thought, and what was coming was definitely a threat.

Marjorie and Charles were a power couple, a pairing of financial giants. In their sixties, they were lean, gym-fit, immaculately groomed. They exuded power. Tom had lost count of the number of boards they were on, of the financial projects they controlled. Together, this couple seemed to run half of corporate Australia.

And here they were, emerging from their crazy-expensive limousine, every inch of them saying, We're here on business.

'Marjorie. Charles.' He made his voice deliberately light as he opened the gate to greet them. 'You've come for Kit's party? I'm sorry but everyone's just left. You've missed the cake.'

'You can still have little red sausages.' Henry spoke up from behind Tom, sounding worried but prepared to be hospitable. 'They're not hot any more but they're yummy.'

'We didn't come for the party,' Charles said, eyeing his grandsons with dislike. 'Although, of course, we knew about it.' That was down to Tom. Every week he insisted the boys write to their grandparents. 'Our lawyers tell us there's been an accident. Weeks ago, and we weren't informed. Christopher's hand. Why did we have to gain access to medical records to find that out?'

'It's better,' Kit whispered.

'It's good as new now,' Henry agreed. 'He cut it while Christine was watching the telly, but Rachel took him to hospital.'

'You weren't with them when it happened?' Marjorie snapped at Tom.

'I was at the hospital. I employed a childminder.'

'Not a satisfactory one,' she threw back at him. 'We've made enquiries. The childminders you're using are unqualified. They've not even undergone the working-with-children security checks. They're totally unsuitable.'

'Rose isn't unsuitable,' Kit said defiantly. 'She's cuddly.'

'According to our sources, she's in her seventies.'

'Could we go inside and discuss this?' Tom broke in. The boys were looking more and more distressed. He needed to get this out of their hearing. 'The boys are playing ball. We'll be better discussing this in private.'

'There's no discussion. We're here to take the boys home,' Charles decreed. 'According to legal advice, our challenge will be successful. Learning of Christopher's cut hand was the last straw. Your care is marginal, to say the least. We're the boys' grandparents. We're in a position to give them professional after-school care, as well as sending them to the best educational institutions. The idea of them attending a hick elementary school here, with heaven knows what sort of teaching, is unthinkable. You're not married. You employ unqualified childminders. You obviously can't keep them safe. You need to allow us to take them now, and if you deny us we'll make sure you have no access. Plus,' he added, almost as an afterthought, 'we'll ruin you.'

'But we don't want to go with you,' Marcus muttered, brave words but with a tremble beneath them. 'You're mean. Mum said Tom would always look after us.'

'She didn't mean live with him,' Marjorie snapped. 'You'll have your own bedrooms in our wonderful home. You'll have a nanny to take care of you. You will need to keep up with your studies but that's no problem. You know we hired a suitable tutor for Christopher...'

'He didn't like his tutor,' Marcus quavered. 'He hit him on the fingers with his pen when he got his spelling wrong. And once when he got them wrong twice he hit him really hard.'

'Then Christopher needs not to get them wrong,' Marjorie said. 'Don't be a baby, Marcus. You know you belong in our world. It's where your mother was raised.'

'Mum hated it there.' Marcus was starting to cry, his voice becoming choked. 'She said you were always away. She said her violin teacher used to hit her fingers, too.'

'For heaven's sake. Your mother didn't make the most of the advantages we offered her but I didn't think she was stupid enough to talk of such foolishness to her children.' Marjorie's voice was turning shrill but Charles laid a placating hand on her shoulder.

'Keep it calm, Marjorie. Heaven knows what these children have been told, by their mother and by this man, but we know where our responsibility lies. Our role is simply to get them back on track as fast as possible. So what's it to be, Dr Lavery? You put them in the car with us, or you face a court order and legal costs that'll make your head swim. Decide now.'

'We're not going with you.' Kit had started crying as well. 'We won't!'

'Don't be foolish, boy,' Charles said. He took a step towards his grandson and put a hand on his shoulder, tugging him towards the car. Kit pulled away but the grip tightened.

'Let me go!'

And then Tuffy decided it was time to step in. The little dog had been partying all afternoon and had retired to the back steps for a nap in a sunbeam. Now, though, with the boys' voices raised, he'd stumped down to see what was going on. Now he started barking, high, hysterical yips, clearly confused, clearly worried.

And then Charles grabbed Kit and Kit cried out and pulled away—and Tuffy saw his duty. Normally the most docile of dogs, he darted forward and sank his teeth into Charles's shoe.

It wasn't a bite. The shiny brogues were solid and, as a rescue dog, Tuffy was missing enough teeth to make any bite pretty much a token affair, but he managed to grip and hold. Charles gave his foot an angry shake but the dog's hold firmed.

'Get the damn thing off me,' he snapped.

Tom lunged forward but, before he could reach dog or child, Charles tried another tack. He set his foot down, then pulled back his other foot and kicked. Hard.

The little dog flew six feet away and landed with a sickening thud on the gravel in front of the car. For one appalling moment he lay totally motionless. Then, as Charles stepped towards him—to kick him again?—he struggled to his feet and headed out of the gate. He was around the fence and into the bushland at the back of the house, and he was gone.

With three boys running after him.

'Get back here!' Charles roared and made to go after them, but Tom gripped him and held.

'Leave them be. Don't you dare…'

And then Rachel was beside him, her tea towel flung aside.

'I'll go,' she said. 'You get rid of these people.'

It made sense. Every instinct told him to follow the kids, but the way Tuffy had run signified he hadn't been badly hurt. The boys were best out of the way while he said what he had to say to this pair. And Rachel was already following them.

'Let me know how Tuffy is, but take your time bringing them back,' he called after her. 'Though probably five minutes is all I need to say what needs to be said here. Charles, Marjorie, into the house. Now.'

# CHAPTER TEN

IT WAS ALL very well to say she'd follow them, but she wasn't sure where they'd gone.

The track around the house led to a path winding down to the beach. She assumed that was where they were, but a fork a little way from the house veered upward. Rachel had investigated once and decided against exploring further. It was pretty much overgrown above waist height—or kangaroo head height—so she suspected it was used by wildlife rather than people.

But now she hesitated. It'd make sense for the boys to have taken the fork to the beach, but they'd been following Tuffy, and Tuffy could have gone either way.

She called and got no answer.

Okay, beach first. She ran, but three minutes later she was staring at a deserted beach. No footprints in the sand. Nothing.

Back to the fork.

She headed up the path, kicking herself mentally for wasting time. It did look as if they'd been this way. The leaf litter had been disturbed, leaving damp ground exposed. The boys were significantly shorter than she was. They'd have got through this easier than she could. Still, she moved fast.

Ten minutes later she was where the path ended, at an obviously little-used lookout giving broken views over the bay. She could see a muddle of fresh footprints but they weren't here now, and all around her was dense bush.

No dog.

No boys.

She stood and called.

Nothing.

There were smaller tracks leading into the bush, but they were surely animal tracks. It was drier up here. There were no tell-tale signs of disturbed foliage.

Had they backtracked? Had she missed them when she'd run to the beach?

Her phone was in her jeans pocket. Crossing every finger and toe, she phoned Tom.

'They've gone,' he said before she could speak. 'I told them they could sue me for every cent I own before I let them have the boys. Heaven knows what'll happen now, but you can tell them it's safe to come home. How's Tuffy? Is he hurt?'

'I can't find him. Tom, I can't find the boys.'

There was a moment's pause. The beginnings of alarm.

'They're not on the beach?'

'Nor up the mountain path. I'm at the lookout. I think they've come this way, but I've called and called and nothing.'

'They'll be hiding.'

'I guess.'

'I'll join you,' he said. 'Give me a couple of moments to ask Rose to come over. I don't want them coming back to an empty house.'

So she stood and waited, staring at the myriad of tiny tracks, agonising over what to do.

If they were indeed hiding it'd be okay. Surely.

But the tracks led into bushland, and the bush was dense. Shallow Bay National Park ran for miles in every direction. These were city kids. If they lost their bearings…

'I'm catastrophizing,' she told herself and forced herself to wait.

Tom was with her in minutes, looking anxious.

'I wasn't sure where to go from here,' she told him. 'There's lots of little tracks but I can't see any sign of which one they took. I thought…if I tried then I might cover up signs…things some-one more experienced can see.'

'They must be hiding,' he said, sounding wor-ried. 'But if Tuffy's hurt… I need to find them.'

He raised his voice and called—the 'Cooee!' that was used as an almost universal cry in the Australian bush. Apart from in movies, Rachel had never heard it—she was a city girl—but it was truly impressive. It echoed out to the bay, and back to the mountains behind them. Surely the boys could hear.

They listened. Silence.

'They must be close,' she told Tom nervously. 'I wasted time heading to the beach first, but I can't have been any more than fifteen minutes behind them.'

'They *must* be hiding,' he said again, but her fears were reflected on his face. 'They'll be ter-rified. Charles is a bully. I've talked enough to Marcus now to know he can use his fists as well as his words to hurt them. Claire told me he never physically hurt her, but she was a girl. Charles is older now, probably less patient, and to be honest I think Claire's death—something he couldn't control—has left them a little crazy. He sees the boys as a duty, to be licked into shape, no matter what it takes. They're not going back there.'

'They don't know that for sure.'

'I don't know that for sure,' he admitted. 'With the legal team that pair has at their disposal…and the fact that I'm single and only their stepdad…'

'The hitting…'

'They'll say I prompted the boys to say it. There's no physical proof.' He closed his eyes to disguise a wash of pain that looked bone-deep— but when he opened them the pain had been replaced by determination.

'Rachel, will you head home? I explored this area as a kid. Many of these paths meander down to the creek. If they reach the creek, they'll see a path that leads one way to the beach, the other into the town. I'll go down now and see if I can head them off. Meanwhile, if you could act as base, backing up Rose… If they get home… I don't know how badly Tuffy's hurt and they'll all need…' He broke off and closed his eyes again but then resumed.

'They'll all need cuddles. Rose will do her best but they'll need multitudes. Can I depend on you?'

'I… Sure.' Cuddles weren't her forte, but in this case…

Actually, in this case she was tempted to go for it right now. So why not?

Because she'd just backed off from Tom's warmth? Because she'd reacted this afternoon with almost as much fear as the boys running from their grandparents?

That's cowardice, she told herself, and Tom was looking grey.

She did it. For the first time in her life Rachel Tilding stepped forward and wrapped her arms around someone.

Not someone. Tom.

'You'll find them, and we'll work it out,' she told him, holding him close.

He put his face in her hair, taking deep breaths. Taking strength? That was fanciful, she thought, but the idea stayed.

'We?' he asked.

'We,' she said, more definitely. 'We'll get this sorted, Tom Lavery. You go find your kids and I'll go home and be ready with cuddles.'

It was a good plan—except he didn't find them.

What followed was a long, long wait, where

Rachel and Rose sat and worried, and Tom's calls back home were increasingly desperate.

'Nothing,' she told him over and over, and as the sun sank he returned. His phone battery was dying. He was exhausted. He needed help.

'I assumed they'd come home by dusk,' he said heavily. 'It's time to call in the big guns.'

Five minutes later a police car pulled into the drive. That was followed by the local fire truck and a State Emergency Services vehicle. Men and women piled out, wearing serious faces and high visibility clothing. Kids lost in this bush meant trouble. No one was wasting time.

Locals were arriving too. Word was out. Shallow Bay was preparing to search.

Tom wasn't allowed to join in.

'No,' the local police sergeant told him. 'And no argument. You have scratches all over you already. You're exhausted and emotional. We're the professionals. You stay here and let us bring the kids to you.'

It nearly killed him, and it nearly killed Rachel to watch him. Like Tom, she'd prefer to be searching herself rather than going nuts with the waiting. But she wasn't even a local. Any volunteer with no experience of night-hiking and bushcraft was being sent home and she knew she'd be useless.

'Come back at dawn if we haven't found them by then,' the local volunteers were being told, and the words sent a chill right through her.

And watching Tom… Watching his fear…

He loved these kids. She saw it on his face and it left her feeling awed.

How could a man take three children into his heart, leaving himself exposed to such pain?

But how could he help it? She was starting to get it, she decided as the night wore on, because the thought of the kids out there was doing her head in. And every time she looked at Tom her own heart twisted.

She didn't do love. She didn't do commitment. It hurt. It was hurting so much now she couldn't bear it, but she had no choice.

Maybe this love thing was something that didn't get decided in any sort of rational manner, she decided. It was a scary thought, but she hardly had headspace to examine it now.

She should go home, get some sleep, Tom told her. There'd still be medical needs tomorrow. It'd be sensible to keep herself grounded, to stay rested and ready for whatever might be required.

She could no sooner go home than she could fly. It was as if her heart had been ensnared, caught in a fine web of...loving?

She was so confused, so fearful, and as the night wore on it grew worse.

It was dark, late, and it had started to rain.

By midnight the police were treating it as deadly serious, and they'd called in the heavies. A helicopter arrived and started doing sweeps, using the house as the epicentre and moving out.

'It has heat-seeking cameras,' the sergeant told them. He'd set up base in Tom's living room. Rose had reluctantly gone home but they could still see her light on. She'd be pacing too.

Half of Shallow Bay seemed to be awake.

People cared.

'The chopper's thermal cameras are our best bet in these conditions,' the policeman was saying. 'Kangaroos make it hard, though. They're about the same mass as a child, so every warm body has to be checked. If we knew the kids were together we could cut out a lot of false sightings, but we can't assume it.'

'They'd never leave each other,' Tom said, his face bleaching even whiter than it had been before.

'If one of the kiddies hurt himself and another tried to go for help...' The sergeant's voice trailed off. 'Well, we don't need to tell you that.'

He headed back to his radio.

Rachel made tea and bullied Tom to drink it. She found some leftover party pies and made him eat them too. She even ate a couple herself, finding some sort of weird comfort in their warmth and ordinariness. It didn't last though. They seemed to sit in her stomach, making her feel ill.

Maybe it was other things making her feel ill.

Every time the radio crackled into life, Tom's whole body seemed to clench. He was sitting on the settee, leaning forward, as if he was willing the radio to give him good news.

Nothing.

Finally Rachel could stand it no longer. She moved across, sat beside him and took his hand in hers.

His fingers tightened on hers, almost convulsively. 'I can't bear it,' he managed. 'I have to do something. I'm going crazy. Sergeant...'

'You're going nowhere,' the policeman told him, not without sympathy. 'Sorry, Doc, but I've read the handbook. First rule of thumb when you're looking for lost kids—or lost anyone, for that matter—is keep their family safe. I let you out there and you'd try and search the whole National Park on your own. You'd end up lost or injured or dead with fatigue. I know it's killing you, but you stay where you are.'

'He's making sense,' Rachel said softly. 'But I want to be out there, too.'

'You'd get loster,' Tom said, with a valiant attempt at humour. It didn't work. His voice broke and that was the end of any last thought of holding him at a distance.

He turned and held her. He just held. Hard. It was as if he needed every skerrick of warmth, of contact, he could get and there was no way she would deny him. She simply held, while the radio spat its stupid static into the room and the policeman toyed with his mug of tea and tried not to look at them. How did cops cope with seeing this level of pain?

'You know what else?' Tom said into her hair. 'They'll use it. If...*when* we find them... Marjorie and Charles... With this level of search, they'll know about it by yesterday. And they'll add it to the list. Cut hand through negligence.

Now lost kids. They'll say it's my negligence and they're right, it is.'

'It's not,' she told him. 'It was them. They scared the boys.'

'Do you think I can prove that? I haven't a hope of keeping them.'

'I might be able to help there,' she said diffidently, and tugged back a little to retrieve her phone from her pocket. 'When Charles and Marjorie arrived... I guess you don't remember, but I came out to find you. And I stopped, thinking I was interrupting something personal, but then you and the kids looked so threatened...'

'We were threatened.'

'Backstory,' she said, still diffident. 'One of the kids I was in care with... Between placements. We were in a home with some pretty rough kids and one of the younger girls was hurt by a couple of bullies. Badly. And I saw it happen but even then there was this code of silence, and the bullies were protected. My word wasn't enough to hold weight. The social workers knew I was telling the truth but there wasn't anything they could do about it.

'But afterwards one of them said, half-jokingly, "You should have had a camera, Rachel. If all the world had cameras it'd make our job so much easier." Somehow, her words stuck. I guess… because of how I react to fear, because there's been…a few other times when I've been scared… if I can't do anything about it, my instinct is to document. It's paranoia, I know, but…'

'It's not paranoia,' he said gently, and he took her hand again. 'It makes sense. So…?'

'So I held up my phone and recorded it,' she told him. 'It was almost a gut reaction. I know it's an infringement of privacy and normally I'd delete it straight away but maybe… I just thought…it might help.'

She held up her phone and clicked on the video she'd taken. She'd been standing back and it was grainy, but there they were, the tableau of people she'd seen as she'd emerged from the back door. The sounds had been caught, too. She'd started recording as Charles had raised his voice, as she'd sensed the children's fear. As voices had grown more threatening she'd started moving closer, in an instinctive move to protect.

The camera zoomed in with her. Charles, large, loud, imperious. Marjorie, shrill and threatening. The two of them speaking harshly, without a word of greeting to their grandchildren.

The children's fear was appallingly obvious. As the tension escalated, the screen showed Charles hauling Kit towards the car. Kit was sobbing in terror, pulling back. Henry and Marcus were looking stunned, terrified. Henry was flinging himself at Tom. Tom was lifting Henry aside to try and reach Kit.

And then came Tuffy. The little dog gripped Charles's shoe, but even on the small screen it was obvious that Charles's foot was uninjured. All Charles had to do was shake him off, but he did no such thing.

The kick was vicious, ruthless, sickening, and the scruffy little dog went flying. There was a moment of appalling stillness while the dog lay on the gravel. Then he staggered to his feet and lurched away, tail tucked under his legs.

The boys ran after him. Charles yelled.

The video stopped.

They were left with silence.

'If anyone dares to say the boys are lost through negligence, I'll personally post this to any on-line forum I can think of,' Rachel said in a shaky voice. 'Tom, I'd go into debt to hire banners over Sydney Harbour if that's what it takes. You're not to blame.'

But he was past listening. He was still staring at the blank screen, as if he could make himself see what was happening to the boys now.

'They'll twist it,' he said savagely. 'Even with this... The lawyers they employ... The bottom line is that I'm single, I'm not related to them. I can't give them the care they can.'

'If you call what they're offering care...' she said and she closed her eyes. 'Okay.'

'Okay, what?' His voice was defeated. Hopeless.

'Okay, you don't need to be single any more,' she told him. 'If it's what you want, if it'd make a difference... You took responsibility for the boys so maybe...' She took a deep breath. 'Maybe I can, too.'

He stared at her incredulously. 'What are you saying?'

'That I might help. That I might even share. If you and the boys need it so much. Maybe...even if we were to be married...'

And where had that come from? The words hung like some sort of threatening sword.

*Married?* Was she nuts?

And he hardly reacted. Maybe he was beyond it. Maybe all he saw at the moment was defeat.

'Tom…' Had he even heard what she'd said?

'You're going to be a radiologist,' he said dully. Help.

She was so confused she scarcely knew what she was putting on the table, but at some level something in her brain was saying it made sense. She was heading down an emotional rabbit hole here, deep and dark, and she had no idea what lay at the end, but the compulsion to help this man, this family, was almost overwhelming.

'I don't need to be a radiologist,' she managed. 'I need to keep your boys safe.'

'Is that a reason for marriage?'

'Hey, it is.' The police sergeant was ostensibly focused on the radio, but he must have been listening in on their conversation as well. He'd visibly brightened. 'This is the first piece of decent listening I've done all night. Take her at her word, Doc. The boys'll have a mum and dad and we'll have two permanent docs for the town. More with that scholarship thing. Shallow Bay won't know itself.'

But Tom was shaking his head, looking bewildered. As if he was trying to clear enough room in his mind to answer.

'Rachel, no,' he said at last. 'It's an extraordinary offer and I don't have the headspace to figure it out, but I do know... You've said you didn't want to be yet another of my "rescues" and you were right. I might care for you—a lot. I also know—even if you don't—that you making this video, focusing on the boys, wasn't you accepting responsibility, it was you caring. As was what you said right now. But you don't know it, Rachel. You don't know what love is and without it...' He raked his hair with his fingers, grim and desperate. 'You can't not let me close because it reeks of rescue and then offer the same thing yourself. You just...can't.'

'But you married Claire without love,' she said, struggling to figure it out herself. 'Surely that was a decision made for convenience? Wouldn't marrying me be the same?'

And that broke through the desolation. He turned and stared at her as if she was something from another planet.

'You think I married Claire without love?'

'You said...'

'I said she was my friend. No, I didn't want her in the way that I want you, Rachel—and don't look like that. You must know how much I'm starting to want you—your body, your warmth, your love. But there it is again. The love word. Claire was my friend from childhood and I loved her. I also loved her boys from the moment they were born. I was their playmate, their big brother, their pseudo uncle, and if you think not being their dad means I don't love them…'

'But you married Claire for sensible reasons.'

'I did,' he agreed. 'But love was behind it. Yes, need was there. Claire needed me, the boys needed me, but if I hadn't loved them I'd be little better than Charles and Marjorie.' He groaned. 'I'm sorry. I'm not making sense even to myself.'

'I don't think either of us are making sense,' she managed. 'Maybe…maybe we could talk about it later. When we've found them.'

'Let's not,' he said heavily. 'Right now, loving's killing me. Loving someone who doesn't love back…' He closed his eyes again. 'Enough. I'm sorry.'

And then the radio crackled into life again and one form of tension was replaced with another. They strained to hear, but it was only someone reporting in.

They went back to waiting. Her stupid offer disappeared into the ether. It was just that, she thought. Stupid. All that mattered was that the boys were found.

Outside, the rain fell as steady drizzle. Somewhere in the hills were three small boys. And creeks that would be turning to rivers. And cliffs, and cold, and fear...

And Rachel sat and watched Tom without touching, and waited, and let responsibility and care and love churn into a chaotic, frightening morass in her mind.

And then, at three minutes past two—not that she was watching the clock or anything—the radio crackled again. 'Sergeant?'

'Here.' The policeman was suddenly sitting upright. There was something about the word, the voice, the tone.

'We think we've got 'em,' the voice said. 'Check the screen.'

The cop swivelled to a computer beside the radio. It'd been showing thermal images of the mountainside all night, taken from the helicopter. Almost before the cop turned, Rachel and Tom were on their feet, staring as well.

They saw search coordinates. Weird, grainy images of bushland.

'Coming around now,' the voice said above the sound of the chopper. And they watched as the coordinates changed, as the chopper flew lower.

And then they saw... Three blurred figures, tiny, beneath the canopy. White, almost ghost-like. Moving while the rest of the scene was still. Jumping?

'Not roos,' the voice said. 'Never seen a roo jump up and down in the one spot. Bit of a clearing a couple of hundred yards ahead. Not big enough to land but we'll send Michelle down on a rope and direct the rest of the searchers in. No promises, but the way the three of them are moving... I reckon we'll have three soggy, tired but well kids coming home in no time.'

The chopper hovered a little longer and they could see the tiny figures waving, trying to attract attention.

And then the chopper moved away, to reach the clearing. The scene was once again thick bush.

'Oh, Tom...' Rachel managed but Tom was no longer with her.

He'd headed for the bathroom and closed the door.

# CHAPTER ELEVEN

THE BOYS WERE brought home in a patrol car just before three. Rachel stayed only long enough to see them sandwich-hugged in Tom's arms. Rose appeared from next door and started fussing about baths and blankets. Rachel watched tears, hugs—love?—and then edged herself out of the picture.

She was an outsider looking in. Wasn't that the way it always was?

'Tuffy?' she said to one of the policemen who'd brought the boys home, and he looked at her blankly.

'Sorry?'

'The little dog the boys were chasing.'

'Oh, yeah,' he said. He, too, was looking at the hugging tableau through eyes that were suspiciously moist. Every person here—and there were many, crowded inside or around the front yard—was soaking up this happy ending. 'There was a dog. The kids had it, but when the chopper flew low it took off into the bush again. The kids were upset about it, but it didn't come when they called and we weren't about to hang around. A couple of the locals said they'd head up there tomorrow to do a search if he doesn't come home himself. I guess he'll come home when he's hungry.'

So Tuffy wasn't messing with this happy ending, but as Rachel made her way back to her cottage he was still very much on her radar.

Along with everything else that had been said this night.

*Loving someone who doesn't love back...*

That one line kept reverberating, somehow intensifying what she'd just seen. Tom, crouching before the fire, holding as much of his boys as he could. The boys, hugging back. Rose, standing beside them, weeping with relief and joy. The searchers, mud-stained, weary, battered from a night of bashing through undergrowth but staying around, soaking in this happy ending. Even the cops with tears in their eyes.

*Loving someone who doesn't love back...*

And Tom...loved her?

How could he possibly? He'd known her for little more than a month. She'd hardly let him near.

Had he so little control of his emotions that he'd let himself fall for someone like her?

Someone who so carefully never loved back?

Emotions were threatening to overwhelm her. She was fighting them back with every tool at her disposal, tools carefully built and squirreled away during a lifetime of emotional emptiness.

They weren't working. Tom. The boys.

And there was a gap.

*Tuffy.*

Back home, she showered—somehow she still seemed to be covered in stickiness from the birthday party—and headed for bed. She shoved her head under the pillow, trying to blot out the emotions of the day. They wouldn't be blotted. Where was the Rachel she'd fought so hard to become? Where was her armour? It was nowhere, and neither was sleep.

At five she was sitting at her kitchen table, staring into a mug of cold tea. At the first hint of dawn, she turned to stare out at the mountains behind the town.

Tom. The boys.

Tuffy.

A ragged little rescue dog. Hurt. Missing a leg. Would he be able to find his way home?

She checked her phone photos and saw the video again, Tuffy flying in to defend his boys against Charles. Boys he loved.

'That's anthropomorphism,' she told herself. 'Giving dogs feelings that humans have.'

Would she have bitten Charles?

'That's anthropomorphism backward,' she said out loud. And then there was another question slamming at her. 'So what am I asking? Can't I love as much as Tuffy?'

There was that word again. Love.

Tom. The boys.

Tuffy.

She glanced out of the window. The house next door was in darkness. She guessed Tom and his boys would all be in his big bed, huddled close. He couldn't leave them.

Her mind went back to the screen shot they'd watched as the helicopter had hovered over the boys. She could still see it. Three white shadows in a sea of unlit bushland. Three spots of heat.

She couldn't remember another heat spot, but then Tuffy was much, much smaller. What she could recall, though, were the numbers at the edge of the screen.

A photographic memory had always been her

blessing, one of her few advantages in her struggle to gain a medical degree. She called on it now. She could still see those numbers. Coordinates.

She wrote them down and then flicked onto her phone. An internet search found a mapping app. She inserted the numbers and there it was, the exact place the boys had been found.

And the app showed her as well. She could see where she was as a little blue blob, with a blue line showing the distance of the blue blob to the coordinates.

Two kilometres. Not so far, but through thick bush...

What was she thinking?

Do nothing foolish, she told herself. There was a mantra given to every trainee doctor, written in stone.

*Do not put yourself in danger when rendering assistance.*

It wasn't just self-preservation, their first-year lecturer had thundered—and he'd been a pretty impressive thunderer. A doctor who put herself in danger escalated the situation to a whole new level, meaning those who came after could be facing a far bigger threat.

But Tuffy was up there somewhere.

She didn't know the bush.

She picked up her cold cup of tea and drank it while she forced her mind towards logic rather than emotion. Be sensible. Think it through.

She had the coordinates. The boys had reached this place, therefore it had to be somewhere she could reach if she was prepared to bush-bash. She had her phone with her app. All she had to do was keep herself—her dot—on the blue line. If it got too hard she could turn back. Her blue line would bring her home.

How could there be danger?

And could she be any use?

Dawn was breaking—just. Tom was stuck where he was. The searchers from the night before would still be solidly asleep. Meanwhile, Tuffy was alone.

Would he stay close to where the boys had been? Maybe he would, she thought, but surely not for long. By the time anyone else came to help, Tuffy could be anywhere.

He still could be anywhere.

She wouldn't think that.

Decision made, she hauled on jeans, windcheater, trainers, plus a rain jacket because it was still drizzling.

She tucked her phone safely in her pocket. Her portable charger was also zipped in. She grabbed a bottle of water and, thinking of a fearful little dog, she added a packet of bacon. What else did she need to rescue one scared, kicked dog?

Luck, she decided. Hope that he'd stayed where he'd last seen the boys.

And if she didn't find him?

Others will come up later, she told herself. I'm not the only one who cares.

Cares?

Loves?

'Quit it with the questions,' she said out loud. 'Just go find a dog.'

Tom stirred within a tangle of arms and legs. Every one of the sleeping kids needed at least some contact. He couldn't move.

The night had wrecked him. He felt drained, empty, devoid of anything except relief that he had them here. They'd arrived home distraught, still frantic about Tuffy, but so exhausted they'd simply slept.

He had to let them sleep now. He was wide

awake, but the moment he moved he felt them cling again. He was their security, their rock, their home.

Tuffy was still out there, a heartache that was yet to be faced. According to a weeping Marcus, the boys had eventually found him before becoming lost themselves. Apparently he'd been bleeding, his back leg damaged, and he'd panicked at the sound of the helicopter.

'We wanted to stay and catch him,' Marcus had sobbed. 'But he wouldn't come and the lady said we had to come home.'

Home. There was that word again.

'We'll find him in the morning,' he'd promised but it was already morning and there was no way he could move. Before they'd left, a few of the locals had agreed to meet at ten and set off to search. It was more than he could expect but ten… That was five hours away.

Then, through his window, he saw the light flicker on in Rachel's cottage. He'd tried to put away the emotions she'd shown the night before, the desolation and confusion he'd seen on her face. He had no time for it, he told himself, but it stayed with him still.

The light he could see was her kitchen window. Curtained. He could see no shape.

Was she thinking over the events of the night before? Calling herself a fool for having offered to marry him? Accepting his explanation that sensible didn't come into it?

They were so different. How could he possibly expect love from someone who'd never had it?

If it was just him, maybe he could take a chance, he thought bleakly. The way he felt about Rachel had taken him by surprise. There was no sense to it. He wanted her, simple as that.

But the boys... A practical stepmother? A woman who operated by rules instead of heart?

Like Charles and Marjorie?

She wasn't like that, he told himself. She could never be like that. But still...

And then Rachel's porch light came on and a shadowy figure slipped out.

Rachel.

The weak dawn light was filtering through the grey. He couldn't see her clearly, but she had a torch and she was heading away from the house. Towards the bush.

What the...?

His phone was on his bedside table. He ma-

noeuvred Henry's head a little so he could reach
it, finding Rachel on his contact list. Her voice,
when she answered, was a little breathless, as if
she'd been rushing.

'Tom?'

'What do you think you're doing?' He was
whispering, keeping still, knowing he couldn't
wake the boys.

'You can see me?'

She'd just reached the edge of the clearing.
'Through the bedroom window. Yes.'

Astonishingly, the figure out there turned and
waved. 'Wish me luck, then. I'm off on a Tuffy
hunt.'

'Rachel!' He couldn't hide the urgency. The
boys stirred. He lowered his voice again, but
it was an effort. 'Are you...? Don't even think
about it. We'll be searching for you.'

'I have a plan,' she said briskly. 'I remembered
the coordinates from last night's rescue. I have
an interactive map, showing me exactly where
I am. I have my fully charged phone and I have
my portable charger for backup. Oh, and I have
bacon and a water bottle. Anything else you can
think of?'

'No!' he practically groaned. 'You can't.'

'I know,' she said softly. 'You want to be here. To be honest, I'd like you here too. But the boys need you.'

'I can't let you go.'

'I need to go.'

'Why?'

'You know why.'

'Rachel, he's just a dog.' He hated saying it but it had to be said. 'You can't put yourself at risk.'

'I'm not risking. Hey, I know... Tom, my phone has this neat location sharing thing on its map app. On my map I'm a little blue dot and I'm following a blue line to where the boys were found. If I hit "Share" I think you can follow my little blue dot on your phone. You'll be able to watch me all the way.'

'Like that'll make a difference.'

'It'll make me feel less alone. I'll feel like you're with me.'

'Rachel...' Deep breath. The urge to toss back the bedcovers and head out there to stop her was almost overwhelming. 'Why are you doing this? It makes sense to wait until someone can join you.'

'And risk Tuffy getting further away? No. Tom, I will be safe. I have my blue line, my dot, my phone, my gear. I have you watching me. But I need to do this.'

'Why?' He felt as if he could hardly breathe.

'Because I love what Tuffy did for the boys,' she said softly. 'And I can't bear that he's out there. I think… I love Tuffy. Love… How scary's that for a confession? Tom, I need to go. I'm sending my location now. You should hear the ping any minute.'

And she turned and headed away, walking steadily until her shadowy figure disappeared from the clearing. She was already on the track leading into dense bush.

He was staring sightlessly at the window. Henry's hand was clutching his arm; he was stirring from sleep. 'T-Tom?'

Had she disconnected?

'Oh, and this love thing…' he heard her say, and it was almost an afterthought.

'Rachel…' Henry's hand tightened in his. He couldn't move. He'd never felt more helpless.

'I can't talk any more,' she told him. 'I need to watch my feet. I just thought I should say… Last night we talked about love. This morning… Tom, I'm not sure what it is but I think I'm learning.'

# CHAPTER TWELVE

THE RAIN KEPT right on raining. For the next two hours Rachel fought her way through the bush. Tom watched her little blue dot and held his boys, and he'd never felt so torn in his life. She was safe, he told himself. Rachel was sensible. She was in communication.

She was alone and he hated it.

It was okay—almost—when she was moving, when he could see the dot progressing. When the dot stopped, his head went straight to disaster scenarios—Rachel falling, broken ankle, head hit on overhead branches, drop bears, antigowobblers... He was going out of his mind!

She knew he'd be worried, though. Often when she paused, she texted.

Bit of a tough uphill. Taking a breather. Still good.

And...

Undergrowth's heavy. Taking a recce to see if there's another way around.

By the time the kids stirred the dot was pretty much where she'd set her destination. Which was good because almost as soon as the boys woke they were fretting about Tuffy.

He showed them the map and the blue dot.

'That's Rachel,' he told them. 'She's gone up to fetch him.'

'Rachel's bringing him home?' He watched their faces sag into relief.

'She hasn't found him yet but she will. She's just reached the spot.'

'But she's by herself.' Marcus was perusing the map with the eye of a scientist, expanding it so he could see details. Trying to see the unseeable.

'She shouldn't be there by herself,' Henry said, frowning. 'We were all together and we were scared.'

'It's light now, though.'

'But it'll still be scary,' Henry insisted. 'We should help her.'

'We could all go,' Kit said. 'We could rescue Rachel and Tuffy.'

He looked at them, his three kids. They were

scratched, bruised, battle-weary. They'd been truly terrified last night. He'd tucked them straight into bed without bothering about baths. They looked like refugees from a battle zone.

They could rescue Rachel?

He looked again at her little blue dot and he thought, She knows where she is. She said she was fine. She was being sensible. She was on her blue line and she didn't need rescuing.

And then he felt the kids around him, the warmth of the big bed, the feeling of the kids depending on him—and, being honest, the way he depended on the kids—and he thought, did she need rescuing?

She might know where she was on the map, but where was she in the world? Did she have a place to come home to?

And then he thought—rescuing Rachel…the word was suddenly topsy-turvy. Why did it feel as if it'd be rescuing himself?

And as if on cue there was a knock on the door. The boys cringed—they were expecting Charles and Marjorie? But it was Rose. Of course it was Rose, bearing a pile of steaming pancakes and a jug of maple syrup.

In two minutes the boys had her up to speed.

She stared at the dot Marcus was showing her and she set her pancakes on the kitchen table and glared at Tom. 'I don't understand dots,' she told him. 'But she's up on the ridge?'

'Yes.'

'There's only one dot.' It was an accusation.

'I couldn't leave the boys.'

'I understand that, but you can leave now,' she told him. 'I'll put some pancakes in foil and make you a Thermos while you pull your boots on.'

'Rose…'

'She's saving Tuffy,' she said. 'She shouldn't be alone, should she?' And then she fixed Tom with a look. 'Especially when you love her.'

'Rose…'

'Blind Freddy can see that you do,' she told him. 'You want to deny it?'

'I… No.'

'Then go,' she told him, and he paused only long enough to give her a big hug that somehow ended up embracing the boys as well.

'I'll ring Roscoe on the way,' he told the boys. 'I doubt Marjorie and Charles would dare to come near us, but if they do… Roscoe will keep an eye on you all. You'll have half of Shallow Bay here to keep you safe in seconds.'

'Then all you need to do is keep Rachel safe,' Rose retorted. 'And find Tuffy and bring them both home.'

But she didn't need to say it. He was already gone.

It took quite a while but she found him.

She'd spent a miserable couple of hours bush-bashing through almost impenetrable under-growth. She'd found the X-marks-the-spot where the coordinates on her phone matched the coor-dinates she'd seen on the screen the night before. She'd found irrefutable evidence that technology hadn't let her down. The clearing she was in was flattened from many boots, churned to mud in some places. There was even a wrapper from a chocolate muesli bar to prove this was where the rescuers had embraced the boys.

No Tuffy.

She'd called and called. She'd gone a little way in either direction, still calling. Nothing.

And then she'd come back to her X-spot, and as she'd sat on a wet log to think, a tiny move-ment caught her eye.

A mound of grevillea lay in front of her, an

Australian native plant with crimson bottlebrush-type flowers and a scratchy, twiggy centre.

She lay down in the mud to try and see under. She shone the torch.

Two terrified eyes peered out at her.

'Tuffy?'

He didn't move.

She tried to wriggle under.

He growled and whined and shrank deeper.

He sounded terrified, she thought. She edged out, trying to figure what to do. If she pushed further under he might bolt. Having him run away was the last thing she wanted.

She unwrapped her bacon and set it under the bush, pushing it until he started backing away. Then she retreated to her log. And phoned.

'Tom? I've found him.'

There was a moment's silence, as though he'd caught his breath and wasn't sure what to say.

'He's under a really big bush,' she told him. 'I can't get him out.'

'Don't do a thing,' he told her. 'Stay right where you are, love. I'm on my way.'

'The boys…?'

'Are with Rose, with Roscoe standing guard. Everyone's safe. Stay still. I'm coming.'

* * *

This was a far cry from the neat, controlled Rachel Tilding he was accustomed to. This woman… Well, to put it bluntly, she was a mess. She was filthy and sodden. Her hair, hauled out of its knot from contact with undergrowth, was full of twigs. Mud smeared her cheeks. Rain was dripping steadily down her face.

Tom broke through the last section of undergrowth and he thought he'd never seen a more beautiful woman in his life.

She was seated on a moss-covered log. She looked huddled and shaky and alone.

She looked up at him as he emerged from the foliage, she smiled and approximately two seconds later, give or take a millisecond, she was in his arms. Gathered to his heart. Held and held and held, as if he could never let her go.

As he never intended to.

She was melting into his body, curving against him, hugging him as fiercely as he was hugging her. The rain dripped on regardless. It didn't matter. There was no need for words. In those first few moments promises were being made, vows formed, ties created that would last for the rest of their lives.

He could feel her heartbeat and it seemed to be in sync with his. That was how it was. That was how it would be.

'I've changed my mind about last night's offer,' he managed, and it was a struggle to get his voice to work. 'I accept. You will marry me. I don't care what we have to do to make it work but it will happen.'

She gave something between a sob and a laugh. 'Oh, Tom…' But somehow she remembered priorities. 'Tuffy…'

Their hold had lasted less than a minute, a hold which meant so much. It felt as if the world had changed. Or settled? It had righted itself on its axis and it was time to move on.

Tuffy.

'He's over there,' Rachel said, somehow pulling back. 'Under the bush. I put the bacon out but he hasn't gone near it. I can't see if he's hurt.'

She was freezing—what the hell was she wearing?—surely not bushwalking gear. Cotton trainers. Some sort of city rain jacket, designed for the odd light shower, not this deluge. Jeans.

He could feel her shaking.

'Tuffy,' she said again, and he thought of priorities and hypothermia but she was standing, pointing at the bush.

Tuffy was obviously right up the top in her triage assessment. A dog who'd saved his kids.

She was the woman who'd saved his dog.

First things first. He hauled off his oilskin and draped it round her shoulders. 'Get that wet top off and get into this,' he told her. 'Now.'

Something in the tone of his voice stopped her protests. She complied while he grabbed the torch and peered under the grevillea.

And there he was. The source of all the trouble.

No. He wasn't trouble, Tom thought. He was simply a little dog who'd brought joy, who'd done what he could.

'Tuffy,' he said.

Rachel's bacon was within reach. He pushed it a little way forward.

Tuffy was a rescue dog. He'd been mistreated in the past. Teaching him to trust had been huge.

It was a big ask now. Rachel hadn't been able to manage it, but then Tuffy didn't know Rachel all that well.

Could he trust now?

'Tuffy,' he said again, and the dog stirred and whined.

'Come on out,' he said gently. 'Come on, mate. We have bacon and we have warmth and we have Rachel. We'll keep you safe. Come on home.'

And, as if he understood, the little dog stirred and wriggled forward, slowly, tentatively. He reached the bacon and sniffed and Tom thought he might grab it and retreat.

But then he wriggled forward a little further. And sniffed Tom's fingers. And made a decision.

He was suddenly out from under the bush, on Tom's knees, every fibre of his small scruffy body wriggling in relief and doggy joy.

And Tom picked him up—and the bacon—and carried him back to Rachel on her log.

And hugged them both for a very long time.

Promises had already been made, deep and abiding. On the trek back to the house they were made again.

Tom had Tuffy tucked under his sweater. The little dog had a nasty gash on his hind leg but he seemed otherwise okay. Full of bacon and one of Rose's pancakes, nestled against Tom's chest, he was where he wanted to be.

As was Rachel. Tom had her hand. He wasn't letting her go for a moment. He was leading her down the mountain, treating her as the most precious thing in the world, and it was okay by her.

Life was okay. Her teeth were still chattering. Tom's coat was keeping the worst of the cold at bay, but the damage had already been done. She was soaked, shivering, but Tom was holding her and she'd never felt so happy in her life.

'We'll get married soon,' Tom said. They'd hardly spoken—Tom was focusing on his feet, on the path ahead, on his job to get them all safe and warm as soon as possible. But he said those four words and Rachel let them sit for a while, savouring them.

Knowing she should think about it. She should be sensible.

'Yes please,' she said, and he tugged her closer and kissed her fiercely on the mouth.

And that was her fate sealed, she thought as he led her on. Just like that, her armour had disappeared.

Just like that, Rachel Tilding decided that she'd fallen in love. And she'd fallen in love for ever.

An hour later she was dressed in a pair of Tom's jogging pants and an oversized singlet. Tom was towelling her hair while the boys fussed over

Tuffy and Rose heated soup. It was almost a dream setting, Rachel thought—Tom's towelling, the way his hands touched her neck with each downward stroke, the warmth of the room, Rose's fussiness…the care…

And suddenly Marcus looked up, focusing on what Tom was doing. Focusing on Rachel.

'What are those things on your arms?' he asked, frowning in sudden concern.

'They're scars,' she told him but then as he kept frowning—Marcus knew by now what scars meant—she struggled through her mist of fuzziness, of peace, of home, to find an explanation.

'When I was little I had to face a dragon,' she told him. 'It wasn't a real dragon but that's what it felt like. So these scars are little dragon teeth burns—see, they're all the same? But you know what I did? I fought my dragon. Back then I fought by myself but now I realise I don't have to. Because people who love you always come to your rescue. Like you went to rescue Tuffy last night, and Tom came to rescue me. People who love you chase away your dragons and you don't have to worry any more.'

'Wow.' Henry rose to inspect the scars and was impressed. 'Dragon teeth!'

'That's better even than crocodile teeth,' Kit decreed. 'Cool!'

'I wish I had dragon teeth on my arms,' Henry said. 'You're really lucky.' But then he hesitated. 'I expect they hurt when you got them.'

'They did a bit,' Rachel said, drifting back under the warmth of the towel, the gentleness of Tom's hands. 'But I'm lucky. I guess… I seem to have found so many people who'll scare away any imaginary dragon who comes near. I've seen your video game. You guys seem to be experts.'.'

'I'll chase away your dragons,' Henry said stoutly.

'And me,' Kit said. 'And Tuffy will help.'

'Me too,' Marcus said, though she could see, at ten, he was a little more dubious about the dragon teeth explanation. 'I guess…whatever it is we'll chase it away together.'

'I'm in, too,' Rose declared from the kitchen. 'Let any dragon come near us and I'll tell them what's what.' The boys giggled. The vision of plump, aproned Rose fending off dragons had them all chuckling.

'What about you, Tom?' Marcus said, figuring there had to be a full set. 'Will you fight for Rachel?'

'Most definitely,' Tom said, settling a kiss on her hair. 'Any dragon comes near this lady and he'll meet a fiery end. All of us will make sure of that. We're your family, Rachel Tilding.' And then, maybe because he thought there'd never be a better time to say it, he tilted her chin and stooped to kiss her.

'So what about it, Our Rachel,' he said softly, lovingly, with all the tenderness in the world. 'Now you're warm and dry, now we're back in the real world. Let's make it formal. I know it's crazy. I know it's way too soon. But what the heck… Will you marry us?'

'What? All of you?' She could hardly speak. She had every set of eyes in the room on her, including Tuffy!

'Yes!' Marcus yelled and whooped. And then he paused. 'But I won't be a pageboy. One of the boys at school says pageboys have to wear velvet suits. Yuck.'

'I don't like velvet suits,' Henry said worriedly, and Rachel couldn't help herself. This was supposedly the most romantic moment of her life and she found herself giggling.

But Tom was face to face with her, and his eyes were still questioning. This was a serious moment. It needed a serious answer.

Would she marry…all of them? Would she cast the last of her armour off and step into this strange, wonderful world of loving?

'Meerkats,' she said, and Tom blinked.

'Pardon?'

'If we can have all you boys wearing meerkat T-shirts at our wedding, then the deal's done,' she told him. 'And maybe I can sew a little meerkat coat for Tuffy.'

'Hooray!' the boys yelled, and Tom kissed her.

And then Rose bustled in with soup, and Tuffy yipped his excitement—and the rest of their lives started right there.

\* \* \* \* \*

# LET'S TALK

# Romance

For exclusive extracts, competitions and special offers, find us online:

**f** facebook.com/millsandboon

**⊙** @millsandboonuk

**🐦** @millsandboon

Or get in touch on 0844 844 1351*

For all the latest titles coming soon, visit millsandboon.co.uk/nextmonth